'Who are you?

'Harriet Logan, siste[...]
And with that out [...]
might tell me what's wrong. I'll put your
tetchiness down to pain—are you ill or
injured?'

James stared at the woman who at first glance
had looked so like Rosemary, his ex-girlfriend,
except that Rosemary would never have
allowed her red-gold curls to spring about her
head in disarray.

'I'm not a patient, I'm the doctor,' he
replied crossly.

Dear Reader

The remnants of gold-rush towns, some deserted, some
still inhabited, are scattered throughout the length and
breadth of Australia. A visit to one of these areas
prompted the writing of this book, so, although Gold
Creek and Hillview don't exist, there are many small
towns like them which still survive, and many prospectors
wandering the hills—looking for 'the big one'. These
days, the new 'gold' is mainly from tourists—travellers
who come to walk with the ghosts of the past, to marvel
at rivers diverted from their course by the labour of five
thousand hopeful prospectors, to peer into holes dug
hundreds of feet down into the earth without the aid of
machinery.

Children pan for gold on the banks of the creeks, while
overhead the kookaburra laughs at their endeavours.
These places are part of our heritage, for without the
discovery of gold the colony of Australia could have
foundered. Where the 'diggers' went, commerce
followed, so towns sprung up, some dying when the rush
moved on, some remaining to serve the folk who stayed
behind to farm the hills left scarred by mines, to run their
sheep and cattle where once a street of shanties stood.
These towns, pinpoints on a map, have their share of
weddings. I hope you enjoy this one.

Meredith Webber

WEDDING AT GOLD CREEK

BY
MEREDITH WEBBER

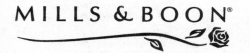

MILLS & BOON®

MILLS & BOON and MILLS & BOON with the Rose Device are registered trademarks of the publisher.

First published in Great Britain 1998
Harlequin Mills & Boon Limited,
Eton House, 18-24 Paradise Road, Richmond, Surrey TW9 1SR

© Meredith Webber 1998

ISBN 0 263 81074 7

Set in Times Roman 10½ on 11 pt.
03-9808-54912-D

Printed and bound in Norway
by AiT Trondheim AS, Trondheim

CHAPTER ONE

HARRIET LOGAN was pushing the last of the clean sheets into the linen cupboard when the phone rang. She shut the doors hurriedly and turned to answer it, then muttered an expletive into the phone as sheets and towels came tumbling out behind her.

'Harry, is that you? Harry, what's wrong?' She moved the phone a little further from her ear to protect her eardrum.

'Yes, I'm here and there's nothing wrong. Apart from the fact that the wretched cupboard has decanted its contents for the second time in ten minutes. And please remember we do have a phone line between us, Doug, so you don't have to bellow like a bull.'

'You're upset,' Doug said, sounding quite pleased by the thought. 'I knew you'd miss me when I left. Have you changed your mind, Harry?'

Harriet sighed, drew a deep breath, then said slowly and carefully, 'I am not upset. You've only been gone since Friday and you're never here at weekends so, no, I'm not missing you and, no, Doug, for the one hundred and eighty-first time, I will not marry you. In fact, I don't think I'll ever marry anyone. I'm destined to be a vinegary old spinster who's pointed out to tourists as one of the landmarks of historical interest at Gold Creek.'

'You a vinegary old spinster? Never!' Doug assured her loyally but Harriet felt his words lacked conviction.

'When are you off?' she asked to change the subject, then she held the receiver even further from her ear as Doug's stentorian voice rose with his enthusiasm.

'Well, if you're leaving in five minutes you'd better

get going. Good luck,' she said when he paused for breath. 'Goodbye, Doug.'

She cut off his final words, knowing full well what they'd be and unwilling to say no for the one hundred and eighty-second time.

How could he imagine she'd marry him when there wasn't even a flutter of attraction between them? A convenience, that's all she'd be to Doug. A good scout. A mate! He even called her Harry—never Harriet, or dear, or darling! She shoved the clean linen back into the shelves with unnecessary force and was trying to wedge the doors shut with a folded piece of paper when the phone summoned her again.

As she reached across the front desk to lift the receiver she heard the soft sighing flutter of falling linen and bit back the word she'd like to have said.

'Gold Creek Surgery.'

'Me again, Harry. I've got to rush because I'm running late now. I forgot to tell you Dan Craven couldn't make it so I got another bloke—he's called Hepworth.' Doug paused, then added in a rich plummy accent, 'Chap I went through school with, actually, James William Alexander Hepworth.'

James William Alexander Hepworth winced as the very expensive undercarriage of his very expensive new Mercedes coupé dragged across yet another lump of vicious ironstone. His hip and leg ached from the jolting even the best-sprung vehicle couldn't control, while words like 'madness' and 'idiocy' clashed in his head.

When he'd realised he needed to work or go insane with the enforced inactivity of convalescence, the idea of a locum's job had been appealing—until he'd faced up to the fact that he probably wasn't fit enough for full-time work and very few doctors were seeking part-time locums. Then he'd seen Doug Watson's name in the sporting pages and had rung him on the offchance that his country practice might offer something he could handle.

He was thinking of Doug's reaction to that phone call when the strip of bitumen appeared, a very thin strip to be sure but enough to ease the tension in his body and let a soft sigh of relief filter from his lips. He even found himself admiring the avenue of dark old cypress pines, forming an arch over the narrow road.

Doug had roared with laughter and protested that life in the bush would never suit him.

'Why,' he'd said, 'for a start, the surgery's a tumbledown shack—no mod cons in Gold Creek—and it's in the middle of nowhere. Apart from that, there's only one unattached female under fifty within a radius of a hundred kilometres and she's mine—my nurse, in fact.'

Unfortunately, he'd ignored the bit about the 'middle of nowhere' and, far from putting him off, the thought of a full month without females, fussing over him and pressing sympathy his way, was very appealing. So much so that he'd not listened properly to the other negatives Doug had listed. Had rough gravel roads been one of them?

'Serves me right for never appreciating how dreadful hospitals are from the patient's side of the bed,' he muttered, concentrating on the road and wondering if he'd come too far.

Take the first turn left, Doug had told him, but the road continued on through the shadowy green gloom, and the stillness of that natural tunnel made him wonder if he'd strayed into another dimension.

He missed the turn, a narrow track snaking left between the trees, cutting back at such an angle it ran almost parallel to the road. Backing up, he manoeuvred around the bend and found the world beyond the trees flooded by bright morning light. The track wound to the right, climbed higher, then dropped to the right again, past a scattering of ancient houses and vacant lots where fruit trees had run wild.

The words 'ghost town' fluttered in his mind and his imagination filled the vacant lots with slab huts and peopled the streets with the bustle of folk brought over the rugged mountains by the lure of gold—the promise of riches beyond their dreams—gold fever! The town had been built on the hillside above the creek that had given it its name, and the distance between the remaining brick and timber dwellings told him it had once been a large settlement.

'The first place on the right', Doug's description of the clinic, finally appeared but James continued until he found a place to turn the car then drove back to park in front of the dilapidated building. He looked around him, this time seeing Gold Creek as it really was—a handful of houses so far apart from each other they exaggerated the loneliness of the surrounding countryside.

Prosperous sheep country stretched for hundreds of miles beyond the hills sheltering the village, and less than an hour's drive to the east would take him to a well-known wine-producing area, but knowing these things intellectually did little to change the feeling that he'd fallen into a time warp.

'Madness' and 'idiocy' were no longer strong enough words. Folly such as his in deciding to take this locum needed words of greater magnitude and strength, but he couldn't think of any offhand so he sighed again and opened the door. He slid his good leg out from under the steering-wheel then shifted in the seat and lifted out his aching left leg to join its mate.

'Bloody useless imbecile,' he muttered to himself.

Harriet had heard the car pull up outside and had assumed it was the locum as patients rarely came on time and never arrived early. She turned from the stock cupboard where she was still fighting with the clean linen, but she couldn't see much through the lace curtains that hung across the wavy old glass of the windows.

Shoving the last sheet in on top of the stack, she shut the door quickly before the whole lot could come tumbling out again. Heritage-listed buildings were a great enticement for tourists, but uneven floors made even the simplest of tasks more difficult. If she found time later she'd wedge another piece of paper under the front legs of the cupboard.

Two paces took her to the front door, which she pulled open in welcome. Welcome? She blinked in disbelief at the sight of the sleek red sports car parked outside. In these parts it looked as alien as a spacecraft. Not the locum after all, she decided. A tourist in trouble or someone who'd become hopelessly lost, looking for the vineyards twenty miles away.

'Can I help you?' she called, and the man who'd been leaning against the dust-covered vehicle turned slowly.

Even from a distance of twenty feet Harriet could see the blood draining from his face. She raced to his side and slid her shoulder beneath his arm to take some of his weight.

'Here, sit back down in the car and get your head between your legs,' she suggested briskly.

'I am not going to faint!' The words were delivered with forceful deliberation and Harriet wondered if his will-power was strong enough to control his autonomic nervous system.

'Then I'll help you into the surgery,' she said, resisting an impulse to offer a wager on the fainting.

He pulled away from her and she felt his strength returning as slack muscles firmed.

'I can manage on my own,' he told her, shifting so his body no longer leaned on hers.

The icy edge to the words warned her not to argue, but warnings had never meant much to Harriet Logan and her resistance to impulses had never been notable for its strength.

'Want to bet?' she asked, smiling cheekily up into the dark and, now she noticed it, undeniably handsome face.

He scowled in reply, golden brown eyes shooting sparks of loathing.

'I don't bet,' he responded, bringing new meaning to the words 'quelling tone'.

'Not bet, when it's the great Australian pastime?' Harriet teased, at the same time manipulating her hip up against the injured man so she could take most of his weight if he did fall.

'I thought drinking was the great Australian pastime,' he muttered moodily, but he accepted her support, and when she moved he moved with her.

'This is damn ridiculous!' The words whistled through teeth Harriet guessed would be clenched in pain.

'Come on,' she encouraged, 'we're nearly there. Although I agree with the "ridiculous"! I don't know what it is with you men that you won't admit to being ill or needing help. We could have done this a lot easier if you'd waited by the car and I'd brought out a wheel-chair. It's not much of a wheelchair but it's got the requisite four wheels and a seat so it would have done the job.'

And why are you twittering on like a demented budgie? she asked herself as she helped the stranger up the two steps and into the waiting room. You've had to half carry ill or intoxicated men before today and haven't felt obliged to give a running commentary.

She bent her knees to lower him towards a chair and felt his sudden heaviness as his will-power lost the battle with his pain and he slumped. A quick twist of her body directed his into the chair and her hands reached out to push his head forward between his knees.

Seconds later the dark head lifted and his eyes met hers.

'Did I win that bet?' he asked, and a smile flickered on lips as pale as chalk.

'I suppose you made it. I'll call it quits,' she said, but when she smiled to seal the agreement his reaction was unmistakable. His eyes darkened as something akin to hatred flared briefly, to be replaced by a shuttered emptiness.

'Who are you?' he demanded abruptly.

Harriet straightened. 'Harriet Logan, Sister in charge of Gold Creek, at your service, sir.' She snapped a salute, then grinned at him. 'And with that out of the way perhaps you might like to tell me what's wrong. I'll put your tetchiness down to pain—are you ill or injured?'

James stared at the woman who, at first glance, had looked so like Rosemary. Studying her now, with most of his mental functions working, he could see the difference. Rosemary would never have allowed her red-gold curls to spring about her head in such untamed disarray, nor would she have appeared in public with the scattering of freckles he knew were across her nose visible for all the world to see.

And Rosemary's pale brows and lashes were artificially darkened while he was willing to bet—if he'd been a betting man—that this woman didn't have to bother with mascara to provide that dusky frame for her—blue eyes?

'You've got blue eyes!'

He heard the words and knew he'd spoken them. Embarrassment brought an unfamiliar heat to his cheeks.

'I thought most redheads had green or grey or brown eyes,' he mumbled, hoping she would accept this as both explanation and apology and wondering why he felt the need to make either.

Sister Logan didn't seem at all fazed by his erratic behaviour. She simply smiled again—a kindly, warm, wide smile that made him think of log fires and cocoa—and repeated her enquiry about where he hurt.

'I'm not a patient, I'm the doctor,' he said crossly. 'And there's nothing wrong with me, apart from a little pain. I was in an accident recently, and jolting over that horror stretch of gravel Doug Watson had the temerity to call a road has shifted things about a bit.'

Harriet stared at him, then dismissed the first hundred questions she'd have liked to ask in favour of the obvious medical query, 'What kind of things shifted? What injuries are you carrying?'

She paused so he could answer but he turned away, looking around the white-washed walls of the waiting room, his distaste for what he saw so obvious Harriet wanted to hit him.

'I need to know,' she pointed out. 'In fact, if you're any kind of doctor you should have brought your medical records with you. This isn't the city where you can phone your specialist at the drop of a hat. If you need medical help, chum, I'm it!'

Well, at least she'd caught his attention. His head turned so abruptly it was a wonder he didn't add a ricked neck to his other injuries.

'No, Sister Logan, I'm it,' he told her. 'I think I'm sufficiently qualified to diagnose my own ills.'

Common sense suggested that Harriet backed away but the last time she could remember backing away had been in second grade when her adversary had been in fourth. After that she'd insisted Pop taught her how to fight.

'Then what's your diagnosis for this sudden collapse?' she asked. 'If the pain was so severe perhaps you shouldn't be working.'

Her concern was justified, James mentally conceded, but shock—not pain—had sent his head spinning. To have reached the end of that painfully tedious journey and seen Rosemary emerge from the tumbledown shack...

'I can manage the pain.' He spoke abruptly and saw

the disgust on her face before she turned away, muttering something under her breath.

'What did you say?' he demanded, and was surprised when she swung back towards him and shrugged.

'I said, "Great! Another bloody drug-addicted doctor foisted on us!" and I meant it.' Her eyes flared with the pure blue of the hottest part of a flame, and her lips, which had earlier appeared full and soft, narrowed in disapproval.

He frowned at her yet felt uneasy about the accusation.

'Snap judgement, Sister? I don't think a couple of paracetamol tablets are going to qualify me for drug addiction, but someday I'd like you to expand on your theory. Particularly as I've known Doug Watson since schooldays and I hardly think an Olympic sportsman like him would fit your probably libellous description.'

'Libel has to be written.' Harriet corrected him automatically, but she'd regretted the rash statement the moment it had been uttered. Not that he'd been meant to hear her words! 'And I wasn't talking about Doug. He's the best thing that's happened to this area for twenty years. It's just a pity he's such a good archer and takes off to competitions—'

'Leaving you with worthless locums?'

Harriet felt the heat rush to her cheeks.

'I didn't say that,' she retorted. 'And you haven't diverted me from my initial enquiry. What's wrong with you?'

What isn't? James would like to have replied. Not only am I hurting far more than I should be, but I've been confronted by a ghost and shown myself to be far less fit than I thought by practically fainting at this overbearing female's feet! He could hardly tell her that.

'I was injured in a car accident some months ago. Fractured my left femur and damaged my pelvis.' He glanced at his inquisitor to see how she'd react to this minimum amount of information.

She was studying him assessingly.

'Ribs? Chest or lung injuries?'

'Three cracked ribs, nothing serious,' he assured her.

'So it was a side-impact accident and you weren't driving,' she stated, with a satisfied nod of her head. 'I sometimes wonder if I'll remember things I had to study years ago and don't get much opportunity to see.'

James found a smile playing around his lips. 'Well, I'm glad I've been able to give you a little theoretical practice. How would your textbook have treated me?'

She looked startled for a moment, then she chuckled, a rich, melodious sound that brought to mind birdsong on spring mornings. Maybe he was weaker than he'd thought!

'A hip spica cast?' she hazarded. 'Dreadfully uncomfortable things, from all the diagrams I saw. They wrap the cast material around the lower trunk and pelvis and down one leg.'

He watched the colour deepen in her cheeks as her gaze dropped to his pelvis then turned quickly away.

'Surely you didn't have to endure that?' she protested. 'Can they use open reduction and traction to immobilise pelvic fractures these days?'

Her dark-fringed eyes looked anxiously at him and he found himself smiling his reassurance.

'These days?' he echoed. 'Is it so long since you studied, Methuselah?'

Her chuckle rippled around the room again. 'It sometimes seems like it,' she said frankly. 'In truth I suppose it's only...' she paused, eyes cast upward to the ceiling as if a list were written there '...eight years since I did musculoskeletal function as a subject but the orthopaedic ward was one I missed when I was doing hospital nursing.'

'Did you specialise at all?' James asked, finding the

soft, lilting tones of her voice unexpectedly soothing to a man in pain.

'In casualty and midwifery and trauma management,' she told him. 'You see, I always knew I'd come back to Gold Creek and would need to know enough to handle minor injuries and have the skills to stabilise more badly injured patients for transport to hospital. It's only in the last three years we've had a regular visiting doctor.'

She paused and smiled at him, a smile which made her eyes gleam with mischief. 'And don't think you've made me forget your medical problems,' she told him. 'Do you find you're getting pain from contractures when you're sitting for any length of time? Is that what happened when you got out of the car? A sandbag or pillow—'

'Hey, I surrender!' James threw up his hands. 'Yes, I did have pain when I stood up but I think it was from jolting over that damnable road rather than from contracture of the muscles around my injured hip. In fact, a very bossy sister during my hospitalisation pulled and pushed me around so much my muscles had no time to lie still, let alone contract!'

He smiled, and Harriet found the simple rearranging of his lips did funny things to her internal organs—making them jump around in a most unusual manner. She ignored this sign of rebellion from her usually well-behaved insides and frowned out towards the blatantly out-of-place vehicle the man had left parked outside.

'Well, that's hardly the ideal transport for this country,' she said, not caring if he heard her pithy contempt.

'I know that now!' he complained. 'But how was I to know roads as bad as that one could exist only three hours' drive from a huge cosmopolitan city like Sydney?'

She stared at him with frank disbelief. 'Surely Doug warned you. Didn't he know what kind of car you drive?'

Her visitor shrugged his impressively wide shoulders.

'The car's new,' he offered by way of a poor excuse.

'And you didn't think to ask about the roads? You didn't consider that home visits in the bush might mean a trip across log-strewn paddocks rather than a leisurely glide down smooth city streets?' She shook her head—city folk never ceased to amaze her!

'Log-strewn paddocks?' he repeated in such horror she found herself laughing.

'The Mercedes will love 'em,' she said with a broad grin.

But she won no answering smile.

'Doug said nothing about home visits,' he persisted, and Harriet decided the situation wasn't nearly as humorous as she'd thought.

'Most GPs, especially in the country where there's no convenient and expensive after-hours service, do home visits. Doug probably assumed you'd know that.'

She looked at the beautifully tailored shirt that spread across his wide chest, at the soft twill of his trousers and the polished splendour of hand-tooled leather shoes, and her earlier suspicions returned.

'That's if you are a doctor,' she muttered.

'So now you think I'm an impostor?' His eyebrows rose to emphasise the question.

'You could be,' she snapped as her heart reacted to the gold-brown eyes staring so disdainfully at her. 'It wouldn't be the first time some madman has begun to practise without a licence.'

The eyebrows rose higher, dark arcs against a too-pale skin.

'Do I look like a madman?'

No, he didn't look like a madman. In fact, he looked like a dangerously attractive representative of the male species. And with thoughts like that, eddying in her mind, Harriet realised she was losing control of the situation. The knowledge sparked her temper.

'How the hell am I supposed to know who you are? You arrived here in a vehicle that would look more at home on a Grand Prix track, you haven't bothered to introduce yourself and locums don't usually pass out on the doorstep on their first day.' Then her sense of humour rescued her. 'By the tenth day, perhaps!' she added, her lips curling into their usual carefree smile.

He looked slightly startled and Harriet wondered if he was the type of doctor more used to fawning deference from the nurses in his life. And if he was? Tough!

'I'm James Hepworth,' he said. 'James William Alexander Hepworth, if you want the whole thing, Sister Logan.'

Gold lights glinted in those lethal eyes. Was he teasing her? It seemed unlikely, given his irritable behaviour earlier, and at least the name was right!

'No doubt always a James, not a Jim or Jamie,' she said lightly as her reactions to this man continued to unnerve her.

He nodded to concede her point, then smiled with a strange complicity.

'And you? Are you always Harriet?'

She was about to tell him, quite untruthfully, that she only answered to her full name when a loud voice made the lie unnecessary.

'Harry! Are you there? Maud's had another attack. Can you come?'

'On my way, Bert!' she called then turned to the newcomer. 'Maud Simpkins, aged sixty. She's been having seizures I suspect are epileptic but neither Doug nor I can convince her she should go to town for a scan. She'll probably be OK by the time I get there and roar at Bert for fetching me.'

Harriet delivered this information while she grabbed her emergency bag and a sheet of white cardboard. 'Do you want to come with me?' she added, as she locked the door that led from the verandah waiting room into the rest of the house and hung the cardboard, a 'Back in ten minutes' sign, on the doorknob.

'Do I have a choice?' James asked.

She seemed startled by the question.

'Of course! You could stay here and look around,' she told him, heading out the door without waiting for his reply.

'After you've locked the door to the inner sanctum and taken the keys?' He hobbled down the shallow steps and followed her towards a battered old Jeep. Sitting still had stiffened his hip joint and his leg ached with a dull insistence. 'And, no, I don't need your help to climb in,' he added when she turned and seemed about to offer him assistance.

'Suit yourself,' she said, hurrying around the bonnet and swinging up easily behind the wheel. 'Ready?'

Without waiting for a reply, she turned the key and revved the engine into roaring life, then backed the decrepit old wreck towards the road with more gusto than finesse. James held his breath, waiting for the shriek of metal he'd hear as they hit the front wing of his new pride and joy.

'Missed it,' she drawled, with a grin that told him she'd done it deliberately. 'That's Bert, heading across the fields, but we'll take the road in deference to your dignity.'

'My dignity?' he protested. 'You've shown precious little respect for my dignity thus far. First I was drug-addicted, then an impostor. Now I'm being flung around in this archaic machine...'

Her smile widened and he felt her good humour reach out and touch him like a sudden breath of warm air on a cold day.

'Are you always so cheerful?' he asked, more abruptly than he'd intended.

She ignored him until she'd pulled into the driveway of a tiny house set back among huge trees and visible only because it was painted the colours of a daffodil, a vivid yellow with orange trim.

'Does cheerful bother you?' she asked as she grabbed her bag and sprang down to the ground. 'Would you prefer grouchy and unpleasant?'

On which note she walked away, leaving him wondering how he should have responded. He didn't actually *prefer* grouchy and unpleasant, but the two words sure as hell described the moods he'd been experiencing lately.

He reached the house—eventually—and found the woman called Harry, kneeling on the floor, beside a volubly protesting woman of immense size. A wizened little gnome of a man, whom James assumed was Bert, hovered at her feet, twittering excuses about why he'd fetched the nurse.

'This is Dr Hepworth, Maud,' Harriet said, somehow sensing he'd arrived before she'd actually seen him. She performed the introductions then added, 'He's a big city doctor and knows what's what—and that includes not taking any of the nonsense you've been putting over poor Doug.'

James knelt awkwardly beside her. 'I'm James Hepworth and not so big a city man that I can't tell when a woman's been overdoing things. Are you comfortable lying there on the floor or would you prefer to shift to a bed or chair? I'm quite happy for you to stay there, if you'd rather.'

'Got more sense than some who're always wanting to get a body upright when her brain's telling her to lie low!' Maud told him. 'But I'd like a pillow for my head, Harry, and a cup of tea wouldn't go astray, Bert.'

'Now you've got rid of them, what do you want to tell me?' James asked, and saw the quick flash of admiration in the pale blue eyes.

'I'm not the best,' Maud confided. 'I'm overweight and that's a problem that isn't going to go away, but it's something in my head. I know it's there, I can almost feel its shape and size some days, but I'm not sure I want all the tests and hospital business, especially if it's one of them tumour things and they'll cut out bits of it then I'll die anyway.'

James took her hand and swallowed the little lump of emotion forming in his throat. Perhaps he'd been out of general practice too long that such a simple statement should affect him.

'You could have the tests, find out what's wrong, listen to what the doctors suggest, then make your decision,' he explained. 'The main test would be a type of scan. It's non-invasive, which means you won't be cut about or hurt in any way. They'll take a picture of the inside of your head.'

'An X-ray? I had one years ago when I broke my leg on that stupid pulley over Bert's shaft.'

'Like an X-ray,' James agreed, 'only while X-rays show us good images of bone the type of scan you'll have will show what's happening with the soft tissues in your head. It's called an MRI and the specialist can examine the pictures on a screen—slice by slice as if your brain's a loaf of sliced bread.'

He spoke quietly, hoping the flow of words and new information would distract his patient while he finished his physical examination of her. Her heartbeat had been rapid but not alarmingly so, her breathing wheezy but he suspected that was normal and, as far as his fingers could tell, there was no irregularity in the hard boniness of her skull which would point to an undetected fracture.

'I'd like to see the slice that's got my memory on it,' Maud told him. 'I could jot down a thing or two to save myself the bother of trying to remember them later.'

'Do you forget many things?' he asked, but before Maud could reply Harriet returned.

'Here's a pillow—shall I ease it under your head?'

James frowned up at the nurse. The entire house was

only about twenty feet square so she must have heard his question. Surely she knew enough not to interrupt before a patient answered. But, no, she bustled about, settling a pillow under Maud's head, then began to chatter on about the dance being organised at the hotel for the following Saturday night.

Harriet could feel her colleague's anger rising but some strange protective instinct made her want to shelter Maud from his probing.

'Maud makes the cheesecakes,' she said to him, knowing he must think her not only rude but possibly insane as well. 'Best cheesecakes in the district, aren't they, Maud?'

As if she was expecting the question, Maud began to recite her recipe, explaining down to the pinch of salt exactly what went into them.

'Best cheesecakes in Australia,' Bert said proudly, returning with the tea and fussing over his wife like a ant faced with too large a crumb. 'Here, love, let's get you comfortable.'

'She has some short-term memory loss,' Harriet whispered quietly to James, who had struggled gingerly back to his feet. 'But the way she tells it you'd swear she was well into the last stages of Alzheimer's.'

Then, in a louder voice, she added, 'I'm sorry, Maud, but we should be going. You know how it is when we get a new doctor—every man and his dog will turn up with some minor ailment. Perhaps if you're feeling better later you could come down to the surgery and talk to Dr Hepworth there.'

She took the newcomer by the arm and steered him out of the house, feeling his resistance in the tension of the hard muscle beneath the fine material of his shirt.

'I assume you have some reason for your behaviour?' he said, flinging off her guiding hand as soon as they were out of sight.

The ice in his voice made Harriet shiver, but she was

damned if she was going to apologise. She knew these people, he didn't!

'Well, apart from a waiting room full of patients, there's the fact that Maud is something of a talker.' She climbed behind the wheel and watched James William Alexander's face tighten with pain as he hauled himself into the passenger seat. She continued in a deliberately light voice, 'Rumour has it she can talk underwater, and although I've never seen it happen—'

'I get the drift,' the newcomer interrupted. 'Once she was fully in possession of her senses it might have been hard for us to get away.'

Harriet flashed him a smile.

'Impossible would be closer to the mark. If she needs an appointment we try to schedule her as the final patient of the day, then I do an "urgent call for you, Doctor" routine when I feel she's had enough time to be rid of the most pressing of her concerns.'

He turned towards her and, although she was watching the road, she was aware of his gaze on her face.

'Does she bring her concerns to the doctor?' he asked. 'I gained the impression she was afraid of medical intervention.'

'Because she won't go to town for tests?' Harriet asked, inordinately pleased that Maud had been able to tell this man her fears. 'It's not for herself but for Bert she's worried. She hates the thought of him having to cope on his own. She's got this idea that if she's dead some nice widow-woman will snap him up, but if she's just sick she'll be nothing but a nuisance.'

Harriet pulled in beside the little house that served as the medical centre for Gold Creek.

'When she comes to see Doug, it's usually to talk about Bert. He's her whole life, you see.'

James stared at the woman, perturbed by a strangely wistful note in her voice.

'And you?' he found himself asking. 'Is there someone that special in your life?'

The question produced a smile so bright and carefree
it made him wonder if he'd imagined an underlying sadness in her words.

'There are seventy-nine "someone specials" in my
life, Dr Hepworth, one hundred and thirty-four if you
count the population of Hillview as well.' She nodded
to where a couple of old-timers sat on the front steps of
the house, then added, 'And I'd say a goodly number of
them are waiting to see you right now.'

CHAPTER TWO

HARRIET watched her new colleague climb cautiously out of the Jeep, straighten his body and walk carefully towards the house. James had a hint of a limp, but it was obvious only because she was looking for it and, although she knew by the stiff way he held his shoulders that his injuries were causing him untold agony, none of the patients would notice. Score one for Dr James!

She overtook him with swift strides and cleared the steps with an authoritative sweep of her hand.

'Make way for the new doctor,' she ordered. 'You fellows should show a little respect. Now, all of you, this is Dr Hepworth. He'll learn your names when he sees you, and I'm sure he'll soon sort out the malingerers.'

She grasped the doctor's arm as she spoke, making it look part of her introductory speech but actually providing some support for him as he climbed the steps and walked across the old verandah, now cluttered with patients.

'This is Marj Allan, who works as our receptionist during doctor's visiting hours.' She smiled at Marj, who sat behind her desk in one corner, and kept moving.

'In here, Doctor,' she continued with a deferential firmness, unlocking the door, leading him into the hall and steering him towards the small room on the left.

Once out of sight of the patients his shoulders slumped slightly and she heard a hiss of breath escape from his lips.

'You should have stayed here and recovered from your trip,' she scolded, 'instead of gallivanting around

24

in the car with me. Now, sit down before you fall down and I'll get some pain relief. Will paracetamol be strong enough or do you want something with codeine in it?'

He sank into the chair and began massaging his thigh.

'Codeine, if you have it and if you think you can cope with that level of drug-taking in your locum.' His words were ragged with pain but when he glanced up at her Harriet saw something like amusement crinkling the pale skin at the corner of his eyes.

'I guess a slight codeine addiction won't matter,' she said gruffly, as the laughter in his eyes made her legs feel hollow. 'I'll be right back.'

She darted into the old kitchen, switched on the kettle, unlocked the drug cupboard and found the tablets she wanted.

'Here's water for the tablets and there's a cup of coffee on the way. Or would you prefer tea? The patients are used to seeing Doug munching his way through their appointments so it won't worry them, and I think you should have something to eat with the analgesics.'

He swallowed the tablets, drained the glass of water, set it down on the desk, then looked up at her, studying her face with an intensity that disturbed her even more than the crinkly eyes.

'Are you always this bossy?' he asked, and she nodded.

'Always,' she assured him. 'Now, which will it be? Tea or coffee? And how do you have it?'

The smile she'd seen earlier hovered around his lips for a second and then disappeared, replaced by a frown as he pulled the first patient folder across the desk and began to study it.

'Black coffee, no sugar,' he replied crisply, and Harriet walked away, curiously deflated by his sudden mood switch.

James watched her leave, the blue skirt of her uniform swishing across very shapely legs. It's only because she looks like Rosemary that she's upsetting your equilibrium, he told himself as he bent his head and began to read about Mrs Carol Williams. But he remembered the relief he'd felt when she'd sensed his pain and taken control a few minutes earlier, hustling him past the patients as if he were contagious. She was probably a damn fine nurse, for all her bossiness! And attractive to boot!

The thought startled him and he frowned it away. One redhead in a lifetime was enough for any sane and sensible man. Now, what about Mrs Williams?

He had finished a quick skim through the pages of the file when his colleague returned, plonking down a cup of coffee and a plate holding two large fruit scones onto the desk. He looked at the butter, melting into the whiteness, smelt the fresh-baked aroma and found his mouth watering.

'Not heard of cholesterol out this way?' he asked, and was pleased to see a tinge of pink colour Nurse Logan's cheeks.

'I thought a bit of butter wouldn't hurt you this once,' she said. 'Now, do you want to eat in peace or will I send Carol in and you can eat while she tells you about her bunions?'

'Bunions?' he repeated, then regretted the query as a devilish delight lit up her lovely eyes.

'I'd say that's what she's come for. Country practice is largely about bunions and burping, Dr Hepworth—about the little things that make people's lives uncomfortable. Big things get sent to the city for tests, but here people want reassurance and sometimes pain relief and often a sure-fire method to get the new baby to sleep through the night.'

He absorbed the words, realising that the leap from life-saving surgery with the transplant teams to bunions was as disorientating as the time warp he'd felt earlier. Was there such a thing as a place warp?

Dismissing the fantasy, he bit into a scone and wondered how such simple fare could taste so delicious. Across the desk, Nurse Logan moved from one foot to the other, as if only awaiting his next order before she left—with another flash of lovely legs.

'Is there a sure-fire way to get a baby to sleep through the night?' he asked, wanting to delay her departure for a few seconds longer.

She shrugged and smiled at him.

'No, but it helps if new mothers realise they're not alone with the problem, and it helps if we can suggest things they can try. It's mainly a matter of getting them through the first few months—'

'Through that state of overwhelmment!'

'I beg your pardon?'

James grinned at her. 'I remember an old professor of obstetrics we had in med school, describing the arrival of the first baby that way. It's an enormous readjustment for the mother and even when everything goes perfectly there's still a sense of dislocation—a state of overwhelmment!'

Harriet stared at him in surprise. That was exactly how many young mothers felt, yet she'd never heard it described so precisely.

'I'll get Carol,' she said, and swiftly left the room, needing time to readjust her initial impressions of the new locum.

The patient flow went smoothly, Dr Hepworth working down the list and all the patients coming out of the room with smiles on their faces.

'Practised charmer,' Harriet muttered to herself as she renewed a dressing on a child's arm.

'Ah, Nurse Logan!' She turned to see him in the doorway.

'Doctor?'

He waited until she'd finished the dressing and had herded the child back out to her mother.

'I've a patient here who's just pointed out that there's no chemist in the village. Do we dispense drugs?'

'We keep a range of antibiotics, mainly the common ones. Our prescriptions are sent to a chemist in town once a week and he replaces what we've prescribed. Most of the locals go to town at least once a fortnight so they make sure they're well stocked with their regular tablets—particularly things like blood pressure and angina medication. We have an emergency stock of those but if it's beyond our capabilities it's a trip to town.'

'We send sick people over that road?' he asked, eyebrows lifting in mock horror.

'People who live out here have more suitable transport than you, Doctor,' Harriet told him sweetly. 'Now, did you want a prescription filled?'

He ignored her jibe and nodded.

'Chap with a badly infected toe. I'll clean it out but think he should take a broad-spectrum antibiotic to follow up. Do we have something like that?'

'I'd use Ibilex 500,' Harriet told him. 'It's cephalexin and should be used with caution in patients—'

'With a penicillin intolerance—yes, Sister, I have heard of the cephalosporin drugs.'

Harriet felt the heat rise to her cheeks. 'I have to make sure I remember all that stuff,' she muttered defensively. 'You see, I'm here all the time, the doctor only visits.' She recovered sufficiently to remember the patient. 'Do you want me to clean out his wound and dress it?'

James Hepworth shrugged.

'What if we share the job?' he suggested. 'I'll need a scalpel and a probe. I've already used a local anaesthetic from my bag to deaden the area but will want some antiseptic solution to bathe it in, a topical antibiotic powder—'

'And dressings,' Harriet finished for him, then she smiled cheekily and added, 'Yes, Doctor, I have heard of dressings!'

Which won a somewhat reluctant smile from the man before he headed back to his room.

Quickly assembling what she wanted, she hurried into the surgery. A young man, a visitor to town who had phoned to make an appointment the previous day, was sitting on the couch, his legs stretched out in front of him.

'I think it's an ingrown toenail, causing the trouble,' James explained to Harriet as she put the instruments he would need within reach. 'I'll cut what I can away,' he continued, turning back to the patient, 'but when this infection is cleared up you could have part of the toenail removed so it doesn't happen again.'

Harriet was surprised by the matter-of-fact way this new doctor spoke. First impressions had been that he'd speak down to his patients, but he was treating this young man as an equal and reassuring him as much with his voice and swift, sure actions as he was with his words. Yes, his voice was definitely reassuring but working so closely beside him, holding the dish while he cut at the toenail, was just the opposite. Her skin became sensitised to his movements and tiny ripples of awareness fluttered along her nerves—

'OK, he's all yours, Sister.'

The command brought her back to earth, voices and rippling nerves forgotten as she bathed, powdered and dressed the toe.

'If you come back tomorrow I'll put on a new dressing,' she told the patient as she helped him pull a grubby sock over the bulky bandage.

'We'll be gone tomorrow,' the stranger replied. 'Just passing through this way and stopped to see if we could strike it rich!'

'Doesn't everyone?' Harriet muttered at the patient's departing back.

'Do they?'

She spun around to face the doctor.

'Just pass through the town?' he added in reply to her puzzled look.

'Nearly everyone,' she sighed, although why she should feel depressed about this transience today she didn't know. 'Tourists are the new gold these days. People come out here to see how the miners lived in the gold rush days, although they forget there was no water flowing from taps or electricity at the flick of a switch. They ooh and ah over decrepit old buildings like this that the heritage people won't allow us to fix, then they pan for gold in the creek and go back to their city homes, feeling they've lived like the pioneers.'

'Anyone who's driven over that road deserves all the accolades of a pioneer,' James told her firmly. 'Now, from the thickness of this file, Bill Cantwell is no transient. Is there anything I should know about him?'

'Bill's a prospector, one of the last of his breed in this area,' Harriet replied. 'He's gone all modern lately and invested in a metal detector. He has trouble with ulcers on his legs from time to time, hence the thick file, but now he's complaining of a pain in his lower back and I'm wondering if it it's anything to do with carrying the detector around for eight hours a day.'

A flicker of humour lit the dark eyes and Harriet thought she saw a slight quirk of his lips as he asked, 'If you've done the diagnosis why not prescribe as well?'

She tried hard not to, but found herself smiling back as she responded in exaggerated horror, 'Oh, I couldn't possibly do that! What's more, Bill's one of the old ones who won't take off his flannel in a woman's company. I only do above the neck and the four extremities with the male old-timers.'

Again there was that vestige of a smile. She waited for a comment but all he said was, 'Send him in.' She left the room feeling disappointed.

'And you've got to stop watching those legs every

time she leaves the room,' James told himself. 'You've worked for years in theatres full of nurses and never felt a need to watch their legs!' He was still wondering about this new preoccupation when a wizened old man shuffled in.

James stood up and held out his hand but the old fellow inspected him closely, before accepting it and giving it a firm shake.

'That Doug weren't never not good enough for Harry,' Bill told him in a confidential whisper.

While James struggled with the triple negative his patient added, 'Me back's bad.' He gestured to his lumbar region.

'Well, let's have a look at you,' James suggested, setting aside the puzzle of the first statement. 'What movement have you got?'

He gestured to Bill to bend towards his toes.

'Well, you can get much lower than I can,' he told the old miner, watching as Bill put his hands on his knees and eased himself back upright, a sure indication that he was in considerable pain. 'That's great, now I want you up on the couch.'

'I ain't takin' m'clothes off,' Bill warned, and James thought he'd have to tell Harriet she wasn't the only one who suffered from Bill's excessive modesty.

'That's OK. Any problems with your bowels or bladder?' he asked, helping Bill on to the couch.

'Me? Nope! Regular as clockwork. My old mum allus said keepin' the bowels open was the secret to a long life, and I can still pee as far as any of the young'ns at the pub.'

James hid a smile. 'Good for you,' he said, gently palpating Bill's stomach while he listened to an expansion on this achievement. He correctly diagnosed a tobacco pouch in one pocket and a hunk of metal—surely not gold?—in another, but there was no indication of any internal mass or lump that shouldn't be there. 'Now,

I want you to keep your leg straight while I lift it up as far as I can and I want you to tell me when it hurts. Left leg first.'

'Yeah, mate, you got it!' Bill grunted, resisting any further movement.

'So, what have you been doing lately? Lifting anything heavy? Digging?' He repeated the leg raise with the right leg and again felt Bill's resistance when the pain became severe.

'Diggin'? I'm diggin' every day and have been for fifty years. I ain't done nothin' that's different 'cept for sweepin' me new detector across old ground I've covered a hundred times before.'

'And how do you sweep the new detector?' James asked, helping Bill back to his feet. 'Pretend it's in your hand and show me.'

'Well, I hold it in me right hand like this and it's got a little arm rest that tucks under me elbow and I go like this.' He mimed a wild sweep across the floor and James saw his body twist first one way and then the other.

'What does it weigh, this grand new machine?' he asked, and Bill looked doubtfully at him.

'Not much,' he said, scratching at his head as if to stimulate his brain. 'Not much at all. It's got this dandy little box with controls and the battery that sits on the pole, but mebbe five, six pounds.'

'And how long have you been using the detector?'

The old man looked at him, his eyes puzzled.

'Week or two,' he said laconically.

James nodded, mainly to hide a sudden flash of annoyance that the overly cheerful nurse he'd inherited was going to be proved right in her diagnosis.

'You could have disc damage, and the only way to find out for sure is to go to town for an X-ray. On the other hand, it's more likely that you've aggravated the discs between a couple of vertebrae with that twisting motion. Lifting and twisting combined is the most common cause of back pain.'

'But I ain't liftin' much,' Bill protested.

'It's enough,' James told him. 'Now, is it possible to lighten your detector by wearing the control case around your neck or on your belt?'

Bill grinned at him.

'You might look a bit posh but you got some sense for a city bloke! Will that get it better?'

James shook his head. 'Not entirely on its own, but I think we'll leave the X-rays until we know if it does respond to treatment. The aggravation has probably caused some swelling in that area so I'll give you a week's supply of anti-inflammatory drugs. Take one a day, try to rest and come back next week if you're still in pain—sooner if it gets worse.'

He scribbled a prescription on a script pad and tore off the sheet to give it to Bill.

'Yes, sir,' the old man told him as he took the script, 'that Doug sure ain't the one for her. Her old Pop could have told her that but he ain't here, and she don't never take a blamed bit of notice of me.'

He fixed his bloodshot gaze on James for a moment, nodded and took his departure.

James stared after him. As well as a bad back, the old chap had a few loose marbles, he decided, then forgot the cryptic conversation as an anxious-looking woman ushered in a younger woman, clutching a young baby.

'I keep telling her he's got to have his shots but when did she ever listen to her mother? Maybe a doctor can tell her, I thought, so I made her come to see you,' the older woman announced. She looked James over carefully, then nodded as if satisfied with what she saw. 'You tell her,' she repeated. 'Her name's Kate and the baby, he's Shaun.'

'And you are?' James asked, aware he was using his most officious voice to counter the woman's attitude. He noticed the younger woman hide a smile behind the baby's head and saw the gentle way she kissed the downy hair.

'I'm her mother, Betty Pearce. Run the hotel here—good meals every night, cater to the tourists who camp down by the creek mainly, though the locals usually put on a bit of a show on Saturdays and all join in. Not that you're likely to be here on a Saturday, a townie like you.'

James hid his own smile. It was apparent the area bred women with a bent for organisation and the bluntest of tongues.

'How do you do?' he said politely to Betty, but it was Kate he settled in the patient's chair. 'And now you've made sure she and Shaun got here safely, perhaps you'd like to wait outside.'

Betty Pearce looked slightly shocked, as if she'd never been asked to wait outside anywhere before today.

'You'll find Sister Logan out there somewhere. Could you please ask her to pop in and see me.'

He ushered the bewildered lady out of the door and turned back to a now broadly smiling Kate.

'She means well, my mum,' Kate explained. 'And I know I should have Shaun done but I keep reading stuff about babies having convulsions after their injections and I don't want that happening to him.'

James leant back against the desk so he was closer to both her and the baby, and nodded sympathetically, aware that he'd have to tread carefully if he wanted to convince the young mother. In surgery you found a problem and removed it—after consultation with the patient, of course. Usually the patient was happy to go along with the doctor's advice... Or were they?

He began to speak, testing every word before he said it so he wouldn't add to Kate's negativity.

'There is a slight risk from the whooping cough vaccine but unfortunately that's the very thing it's important to protect babies from. Did you also read where three babies, all under six weeks and too young to have been immunised, have died from whooping cough this year?'

'Yeah, that's what freaked Mum out. But Shaun's four months now.'

'He's still at risk,' James told her gently. 'Infants up to twelve months are particularly susceptible to whooping cough. That's why we usually start an immunisation programme at two months.'

There was a soft tap on the door and he looked up to see Harriet enter.

'Kate's concerned about immunisation for Shaun,' he told her, and watched as she approached the pair, clucking at the baby to make him smile then taking him out of his mother's arms and swinging him high so she could nuzzle his stomach with her mouth. His crows of laughter echoed around the room.

'Kate and I have this argument every time we meet,' she said, settling the baby on one hip and wincing as he grabbed a handful of her curls and tugged. 'Stop that, you little devil,' she scolded, removing his chubby fingers. 'I think the best thing would be that if she decides to go ahead I stay over at the pub for the first night in case he does have a reaction of any kind. Then I can be on hand to cool him down or give him whatever is needed.'

James found himself staring at her, the image of the red-headed woman and the laughing infant so poignant he felt a stab of pain in his chest.

'That's ridiculous!' he objected, far too sharply. 'We can't offer qualified nursing support as back-up for every baby immunised.'

Harriet moved to stand a little behind Kate and frowned ferociously at him.

'I'm not offering as a nurse but as a friend,' she countered staunchly, then she handed the baby back to his mother and said, 'What do you think, Kate?'

The girl looked at Harriet then turned to James.

'You really believe the shots are necessary?' she asked him, and he nodded, sorry his words had renewed her doubts.

'I do,' he said, 'and I can also assure you that the risk of a reaction beyond a slight bit of discomfort is very unlikely.'

The girl's eyes filled with tears and she clutched the baby tightly.

'He's all I've got, you see,' she said softly. 'And I'm so afraid for him.'

Surely he couldn't be getting emotional again, James thought as he swallowed hard and turned to Harriet.

'Do we keep triple antigen?' he asked, and she shook her head.

'We order up bulk lots when we've got a few kids to do but don't keep it on hand because it has to be stored at two to eight degrees Celsius and our power is unpredictable. I can arrange for some to be sent to us at Hillview tomorrow and we can make an appointment for young Shaun for Wednesday.'

Once again she had moved out of Kate's line of sight and began pulling faces at him. Was she telling him not to ask why it required an appointment with him when it was customary for a nurse to give the injection and she seemed quite happy to do everything else herself? Including diagnoses!

'OK, we'll see you Wednesday, then,' he said to Kate, and let Harriet usher the pair out of the door.

Harriet reappeared seconds later. 'You've another three waiting and it's already lunchtime so I'll show your next patient in and explain about Kate later while we eat.' She turned on a bright smile and said in a louder voice, 'This is Mrs Jackson, Doctor. Mrs Jackson, Dr Hepworth.'

James caught the glimmer of mischief in the nurse's eyes then forgot Harriet Logan as Mrs Jackson tottered through the door. She could have been any age from sixty to a hundred and was so swathed in scarves and frilly draperies that it was hard to see where the coverings finished and the person began.

'I'm not sick,' a frail voice quavered, and James amended his guess at her age upwards towards the older mark. 'I just like to come and introduce myself to new men when they come to town. You never know if they might be looking for a woman.'

He felt the shock of her words jolt against his spine and thought fleetingly of strangling Sister Logan who must be chuckling into her drug cupboard at this very moment.

'Well, that's very nice of you, Mrs Jackson,' he said smoothly. 'But, seeing you're here, perhaps I'd better take your blood pressure so it looks as if I'm doing something.'

'It'll be one hundred and seventy over one hundred, young man,' she told him, settling herself into the chair and removing the layers covering one frail arm. 'It always is when that nice Douglas takes it. Now, there's a man who needs a woman but he seems more taken with that tomboy, Harry, than he is with me. Still, as my dear fifth husband used to say, there's no accounting for taste, is there?'

She finished speaking as he was pumping air into the blood-pressure cuff and tilted her head up to give him a coy smile. He caught a whiff of peppermint on her breath and, underlying that, the aroma of—what?

'Sherry,' Harriet told him a little later as they sat in the kitchen at the back of the old house and shared her sandwiches. 'Poor dear, she started having a few nips when her husband was ill—said it kept her feeling cheerful and he liked her to be cheerful.'

'Which husband?' James asked, idly watching the way the sun tangled in the fiery curls of his companion.

'Oh, Fred, I think. There were two very close together, Fred and Kevin, and I always get them mixed up.'

She smiled at him and another sunbeam caught the glint of gold in the freckles on her nose and gleamed on her even white teeth.

'Were there really five?' he asked, and saw her nod.

'I suspect there'd have been more if she'd had her way. She's been after number six for some years now but all the old-timers are dying so—'

The words stopped abruptly, the laughter gone from her face.

'She's not potty, you know,' she said earnestly. 'Or an alcoholic. I keep a close eye on her and the Pearces are careful about the amount of sherry they sell her.'

Her blue eyes were fixed on him, as if willing him to understand—not to laugh at an old lady who came in to make advances to him. Not that he wanted to laugh. In fact, he was having so much trouble adjusting to his place warp that laughter was the furthest thing from his mind.

'You're very protective of your own. I can understand that,' James said quietly. 'In fact, I find myself admiring it.'

Harriet stared at him, unable to believe he could actually have said those words. Not that staring at him was a good idea, he had the most compelling facial bones—

'Now tell me about Kate,' he suggested, and she had to pull her thoughts away from the uniqueness of his profile, the forehead, nose and chin aligned as if by some master sculptor...

'I suggested you do the vaccination because I don't think she's ever had a postnatal check of any kind and I thought you might be able to suggest it. I think she feels she knows Doug too well to want him to do it.'

He looked at her in such a way that he seemed to understand—to actually *want* to know more about these people who meant so much to her. The thought brought an accompanying warmth and her voice softened as she went on to explain.

'She became pregnant by her boyfriend while they were still at school. They came to see me and talked about options, discussing abortion quite calmly but wanting me also to help them understand the difficulties they might face if they married and kept the baby. Kate's a very sensible girl and Brett was a great young kid, bright and full of energy and ambition. He'd made plans to go on to university and knew it could all come tumbling down.'

She paused, remembering the long, difficult hours she'd spent counselling the two kids, trying to help them grasp the implications of the decision they had to make. Remembering, also, the night she'd been called out...

'He was killed when his motorbike went over the edge of the back road to town. One of the patients I couldn't stabilise for transport,' she added bitterly, the tears she'd shed over the waste of such a young and vibrant life returning to haze her vision.

'We can't save everyone,' James said quietly, and reached out to touch her gently on the hand.

She felt that touch like a brush of heat across her skin and snatched her hand away. She'd met this man less than five hours ago, yet he was danger. She knew that as surely as she knew her own name.

CHAPTER THREE

JAMES felt his hand drop to the table and wondered why Harriet had so abruptly rejected what, after all, had only been sympathy. Still, if that's the way she wanted to be, why should he worry? He was only here for a month—self-imposed therapy to keep him from brooding too much about the past or the future—a chance to step outside the devastation of his own life for a short time.

'So, what's the programme after lunch?' he asked, sitting back in his chair to show he wouldn't let his hands anywhere near hers again.

'Home visits, if there are any booked, or an early mark for the doctor,' she answered, but her eyes were fixed on a point above his head and the faint colour in her cheeks probably had nothing to do with the heat. What had Doug said about her? She's mine? But James had taken that to mean she's my nurse, not my lover. Somehow the thought of this attractive, vibrant woman with Doug...

If she was involved with Doug would she see even that casual touch as a violation of that relationship? Surely not. He was still puzzling over her reaction—and his own to her—when she continued.

'Actually there's one home visit booked today. It's to an elderly woman who lives with her daughter. She's very frail and has pernicious anaemia. I sent blood away for testing last week and it shows she's due for a B12 injection. Doug usually visits her fortnightly, as much to reassure the daughter, Janet, that she's doing the right thing as to treat the patient.'

She sounded so defensive again that he had to smile.

'Hey,' he said gently, 'I may have been out of general practice for a while but I do remember that one of the tenets of good doctoring is about making people feel better even when we can't cure them. And I have enormous admiration for families who are willing and able to keep their elderly relatives at home. It's emotionally and physically draining but it sure beats most nursing-home situations and hospitals for the terminally ill.'

He saw the colour deepen in Harriet's cheeks and the flash of gratitude in the dark sapphire of her eyes.

'I guess I am over-protective of my patients,' she admitted, 'but I grew up here and I've known most of them all my life. Old Mrs Reynolds taught me to knit and crochet when I was a child and those scones you ate this morning were Janet's recipe.'

She stopped suddenly as if afraid she'd said too much, then stood up and walked out of the kitchen. An unexpected disappointment shafted through James. She had such a soft, unaffected voice that it seemed to soothe and comfort—the perfect nurse's voice.

'Here's Mrs Reynolds's file,' she said, returning to drop a folder on the table in front of him and sweep the remnants of their lunch off the table with crisp efficiency and no visible evidence of soothing or comfort!

He felt the file's weight and ran his fingers over the time-softened edges as she clattered their plates into the sink and washed them noisily, but his attention wasn't on the tattered collection of notes and test results. It was on the woman at the sink, and he found himself wondering about other women who had stood there.

'This house hasn't been altered much to suit its new purpose, has it?' he asked.

'Altered?' She shook her head. 'No way! And don't think I don't curse its heritage listing every day of the year. Some photographer came through here by chance during the gold rush days. He took pictures of the whole town—probably hoping to sell folks photographs of their homes. Fortunately—or unfortunately—those photographic plates survived so the images of the town as it was have been preserved for posterity. Now the Heritage Department has listed all the buildings still standing and the owners are only allowed to make renovations with the department's permission and using the same material as in the original construction.'

James looked around again, seeing the old building in a different light.

'But the kitchen's not original,' he argued, pointing towards the enamel sink with its pitted but still shiny tap above it.

Harriet smiled at him. 'No, we were lucky there,' she said. 'Someone living in the house modernised it in about 1920 before heritage became a catchword. The old kitchen would have been in a detached building out the back because of fear of fires and this room would probably have been the bedroom. The 1920s owner closed in the front verandah to use as a bedroom and put in the tap and sink. The house fell vacant during the forties and the government of the day decided it would make an ideal base for an area nurse. When doctors started doing sessions out here, they had to be fitted in as best they could.'

'You make us sound like necessary evils, intruding into your little domain.'

'Oh, no,' she told him, smiling broadly, 'This might seem like hillbilly country to you but the locals believe they're entitled to the same privileges as their city cousins, and that includes Medicare!'

He wanted to ask more questions but was distracted by that smile, his mind going blank for a moment as he tried to remember Rosemary's smile.

Forget smiles, he told himself. Think about your work. He opened the file and bent over it.

'This date of birth can't be right!' he muttered, frowning as he did some quick mental arithmetic. 'It would make Mrs Reynolds one hundred and four!'

Harriet turned from the sink, soap suds frothing on her hands, and grinned the know-it-all grin that she must have known irritated him. How had he ever found her soothing?

'Not done much geriatrics, Doctor?' she asked, the smile chasing around her lips and drawing his attention to their fullness.

'She is one hundred and four?'

She nodded and the smile widened.

'And Janet's eighty-eight,' she added. 'They married young in the good old days!'

He'd have liked to have argued with her about how 'good' those good old days had been but he was battling to assimilate her second bit of information.

'She's eighty-eight and taking care of her mother? Does she have some help? Are there younger relatives?'

Harriet fished the last of the dishes out of the sudsy water and reached for the teatowel.

'Yes, no and yes are the answers to your questions. Janet manages on her own. There are neighbours who pop in and a couple of friends take her to town to do her shopping once a week while another woman sits with Mrs Reynolds. The problem is they're both fiercely independent and will only take so much in the way of assistance.'

He stared at her for a moment as if he needed time to absorb her words, then he turned back to the file as she finished the dishes and wondered why she was undertaking this small domestic task alone when she would have insisted Doug share it.

Showing off for the new man? Surely not!

'How are your leg and hip feeling? Do you want more painkillers?' The questions occurred to her the moment her agile brain found his injury as an excuse to let him off helping with the dishes.

'No, it's settled down quite well,' he said, and glanced up in time to catch her studying the way his neck disappeared into the collar of his shirt.

'Then what's the plan?' she asked, to cover her momentary confusion. 'Mrs Reynolds lives out along the Serviceton road so you'll be on your way back to town if you want to take your car.'

He looked puzzled, then distinctly unhappy, frowning and tapping at the table with long fingers, complete with well-manicured nails.

'You're not going back to town?' She put forward her guess and saw his confusion deepen.

'Well, I had intended to,' he said gruffly. 'Doug has booked me into a motel for the month. He explained it was no more than an hour's trip out here and that Hillview was even closer, but as I'm only filling in for his country sessions and he's got another locum doing his town work...'

Harriet felt a devilish glee bubbling up inside her as she guessed at his dilemma.

'You don't want to take that useless hunk of metal you call a car back and forth over these roads four days a week—is that it?'

He straightened in his seat and folded his arms, as if rejecting her description of his pride and joy.

'But, on the other hand, being stuck out here in the back of beyond on a permanent basis isn't exactly how you'd pictured your month either.' She knew she'd hit home when his lips tightened and his body became even more rigid. 'Perhaps you could hire a more suitable car for the month and charge it to Doug.'

Which should succeed in irritating both the doctors in her life! With a sense of mischievous satisfaction Harriet leaned back against the sink but she didn't have to wait long for his rebuttal.

'My reluctance to drive back and forth to town has nothing to do with my car,' he said crisply, then he half smiled and added, 'Well, not entirely. I'm more concerned with undoing all the good work the surgeons did on my hip and pelvis by jolting over that horror stretch of road. I'm fairly well on in convalescence so the joint and bone will stand up to a reasonable amount of work but I'd been warned against standing for long periods of time—'

'What medicine had you been practising?' Harriet interrupted when a sudden bitterness in his voice cut through the air. 'Surgery?'

He nodded. 'I'd just joined the transplant team at St Mary's—a beginner with them but with my career on track for bigger things.'

The bitterness deepened to a banked-down rage and it was all Harriet could do to prevent herself reaching out to touch him in sympathy. Not that she thought this man would accept sympathy.

'And what's the prognosis?' she asked instead. 'Will you eventually be able to support yourself for long enough to make a return to that work possible?'

His brown eyes looked bleakly into hers, no shafts of gold visible in the darkness.

'I don't know,' he admitted. 'And perhaps it's not going to be an option. My position has already been filled by another ambitious young doctor. Can you see him—or her, as it is in this case—standing meekly aside when I'm well enough to return—if I'm ever well enough to return?'

Now she not only wanted to reach out and touch him, she wanted to wrap her arms around him and hug him, holding him until that dreadful disappointment eased a little and life didn't look quite so bleak.

She grinned to herself as she considered James William Alexander Hepworth's reaction to a hug from his temporary nurse. Definitely not the done thing, she decided, and said cheerfully, 'Well, there are plenty of other fields of medicine which don't involve standing for long periods of time, although I can understand your disappointment at not being able to pursue your dream. And now perhaps we should consider getting on with the day's work. Will you take your car to Mrs Reynolds or come with me in the old Jeep?'

She watched the shudder of distaste cross his face and said defensively, 'It's a very well-sprung Jeep. You should remember it's the same type of vehicle used to transport wounded soldiers during the war.'

'First or Second?' he asked, and she flushed.

'It'll still be running when your shiny status symbol is a squashed heap of metal in a scrapyard.'

He ignored her jibe, staring thoughtfully out the back door of the small house towards the old cherry plum tree.

'Would there be somewhere here I could stay? The hotel, maybe? That would solve the problem of travelling back and forth across that road four days a week.'

'But you'd be bored witless,' Harriet protested, uneasy at the idea of this man being around any more than his working hours required. 'Anyway, the hotel has no habitable rooms and the only other bed and breakfast place shuts down over autumn and winter.'

'Only *other* bed and breakfast?'

Had she said 'other'? Talk about a Freudian slip!

'Well,' she admitted reluctantly, 'there's one place that has a couple of rooms available all year. The owner does bed and breakfast and visitors can either use the kitchen to fix their lunch and prepare an evening meal or eat at the pub.'

She let the words fall stiffly from her lips.

'It hardly sounds like a warm and welcoming invitation to stay over in this God-forsaken hole but if they're the only rooms available I may have to consider them.'

'Them?' Harriet echoed. 'You want both? You have a family?'

She checked his ringless fingers and wondered why it wasn't made a legal requirement that all married men were visibly identified—preferably by a tattoo across their foreheads.

'No, I don't want both,' he said shortly. 'It was a figure of speech, that's all, and I haven't yet decided what I'll do so let's go visit this venerable old patient of yours in your horror conveyance and I'll think about my immediate future on the way. Now, what do we need for Mrs Reynolds?'

He watched as Harriet unlocked the drug cupboard. There was a small refrigerator set in one corner of it but the Vitamin B12 injections were on a higher shelf. As she found what she wanted he studied the contents of the cupboard. For a not very large but an extremely full metal cabinet, it was surprisingly well organised—but then he had a feeling Sister Logan would be a very organised young woman.

'Who brings scripts from town if we need something in a hurry?' he asked, eyeing the range of 'prescription only' medications on view.

'There's a bus takes the Hillview kids to high school in town so if we need anything I phone the chemist and the bus driver will bring it to one of the afternoon clinics we run there. Of course, Doug can also bring things out but the bus is more reliable.'

'Do you tell him that?' James queried as she locked the cupboard and headed towards the front door.

She half turned to give him a mocking smile.

'All the time,' she assured him. 'It keeps him in his place! Now, out you come so I can lock up here.'

'Yes, ma'am,' he said, but he found himself smiling as he detoured via his 'surgery' to get his bag and stethoscope.

She waited while he made his way stiffly out onto the enclosed verandah then she locked the door and reached out to take his arm as he walked down the steps.

'You should use a stick,' she suggested, and he shook

off her supporting hand, his light-hearted mood vanishing as swiftly as the sun behind fast-racing clouds.

'It's bad enough being a cripple without advertising the fact with a stick,' he fumed, frowning at her abominable car and acknowledging that the mix of attraction and rage he felt towards this young woman was a transference of his feelings for Rosemary.

And, brother, did he have some feelings to transfer. He'd tried not to be bitter, tried not to blame her for the accident that had left her free to take his job while he'd lain trussed up in hospital. But the sense of betrayal wouldn't go away...

Harriet stared at him, unable to believe that misery could be so clearly etched on someone's face. Not pain so much as clearly delineated unhappiness. But his misery was none of her business. He'd shaken off her hand when she'd offered physical support, and he sure as hell wouldn't accept or want any emotional props.

'You actually have to climb into the vehicle before it will take you anywhere.' She spoke brusquely, denying her reaction to this man's distress.

'I suppose you boss Doug around like this,' he grumbled as he lifted himself gingerly into the passenger seat and adjusted the seat belt.

Ignoring him, Harriet started the engine, backed out more slowly than she had earlier and turned towards the lower street.

'Not deigning to reply?' he persisted.

'I'm putting your attitude down to pain,' she said in lofty tones. 'Now, just along here is Mrs Reynolds's place. Janet's very proud of her garden so make sure you mention—'

She caught herself in the act and turned to smile at him.

'I guess I must be bossy,' she admitted. 'Comes with the territory, I suppose, spending all my life telling people to take this or do that—for their own good, of course.'

He was startled by her admission. She could see it in his eyes—surprise and something else that made her feel warm and slightly uncomfortable.

'It's a very beautiful garden,' she said awkwardly. 'A cottage garden which grew around a cottage, not one especially planted to look cottagey.'

He nodded and when she stopped outside another ancient bungalow he eased himself out and walked towards the gate, pausing to admire the riot of colour spilling out on either side of the front path.

'If only the city dwellers who aim for this effect could see the real thing,' he said, loudly enough for the woman who had opened the front door and was waiting to welcome them to hear.

'Not bad for a new chum,' Harriet murmured as she followed him down the path. 'But you'd better brace yourself for the inside.'

She introduced him to Janet then preceded him into the house, turning when she reached the safety of the lounge room to see his reaction. The cottage was cluttered with furniture, ferns, hand-crafted knick-knacks and mementos and memorabilia, reaching back three generations. China dogs waged silent war with sleek crystal cats, while stuffed birds of every colour and breed peered down from the mantel and a curiously shaped mug bearing the words HAVING A GOOD TIME IN BRIGHTON stood beside a polished brass shell, the type that had been brought back as a souvenir from the First World War.

'What a lot of treasures you have,' James said in admiring tones and Harriet gave him a mental tick for good behaviour. But when his eyes met hers and she saw the laughter brimming in them she rescinded the tick, knowing he was suppressing his delight while trying to make her disgrace herself by laughing.

'And Mrs Reynolds? Where is she?''

He peered around the room as if his patient might be hidden somewhere among the lace doilies and maidenhair fern.

'Oh, she's through this way—in her bedroom,' Janet told him, leading him along a narrow path through the furniture to a wide bedroom at the back of the house. 'She likes to be in here with her things around her. And you have to yell because she's a bit deaf.'

Harriet hovered in the background while Janet yelled the introduction, then she propped herself against the doorjamb and watched the new locum in action. He had charm, she'd give him that. And skill, she conceded as he examined Mrs Reynolds, talking directly to her all the time but using his hands and eyes to assess her physical status.

In spite of his size and very overt masculinity, he seemed quite at home in this extremely feminine bedroom with its lace-edged pillows, lace curtains and flower-sprigged upholstery and bedspread. In fact, the contrast was exotic and—

'Mrs Reynolds's injection please, Sister.'

She snapped her mind back into work mode and fished in her bag, hastily pulling out the swabs, antiseptic solution and the prepared injection. She set them in a kidney dish she always carried and put it on the tray Janet had ready on a table by the door, then carried the lot across to the bed and held it for James.

Mrs Reynolds smiled at her and reached out to touch her arm.

'You're well, Harriet?' she asked in her soft, tired voice.

'Very well, Mrs Reynolds,' she replied, smiling and nodding to convey the message in action as well as words.

'He seems a nice young man,' the old lady continued, and Harriet bit back a smile and looked studiously away from James who was removing the protective cover from the needle.

'He does, doesn't he?' she replied, hoping her agreement would swing their patient to another subject. But no!

'Not as good-looking as Doug, of course,' Mrs Reynolds continued, and Harriet shifted her gaze back to the doctor, puzzled by the statement.

She'd never thought of Doug as good-looking although she supposed some people might find his straight features, bright wheat-coloured hair and sunny blue eyes attractive. However, this was hardly the time to tell Mrs Reynolds she preferred dark men with haunted brown eyes that could lighten to a warm treacly colour when he smiled. She was still lost in her ruminations when Janet rescued her.

'You don't think anyone's as good-looking as Doug,' she told her mother. 'It's because Dad was fair you go for fair men.'

The subject of this bizarre conversation seemed totally unperturbed by it, preparing the injection then siting it carefully, moving the wrinkled old skin aside with the needle before sliding it into the stringy muscle on Mrs Reynolds's buttock.

'Stops it all leaking back out if we have the hole in a slightly different place,' he explained as he did it, and Harriet wondered how much general practice he'd done for such minor details and skills to remain with him.

The visit ended with an offer of tea and only Harriet noticed the slight shudder that ran through James's lanky frame as he made a polite excuse and bade the two women goodbye.

'I'd have knocked something over if I'd had to sit down in that living room and attempt to balance a cup of tea on my knee,' he admitted when they reached the car. 'I doubt there'd have been room to stretch my leg, and it still cramps up and behaves unpredictably at times.'

Harriet smiled. 'You should be honoured you were asked,' she told him. 'Doug might be better looking but he's never asked to take tea with them.'

James noticed the laughter gleaming irrepressibly in her eyes and returned her smile.

'Is he better looking?' he asked, unable to resist an urge to tease her.

She studied him for a moment and he regretted the impulse, not wanting her to find him lacking in any way.

'Well, he's bulkier than you and has that open, country kind of face, but I think I prefer the dark, lean and hungry look myself.'

Her eyes challenged him to decide if she was telling him the truth or simply pandering to his ego, but a sudden wave of tiredness—and an awareness of the pain in his injured body—brought the game to an end.

'Come on,' she urged, again registering the exact moment when he'd overstretched himself. 'Let's get you home.'

'I don't have a home,' James grumbled as he let her help him into the Jeep. 'I drove straight out here from the city so at least my clothes are still in the boot of the car.'

She smelled of roses, or were there roses in the garden? Exhaustion was confusing him, or this woman who knew when he hurt was bewitching him in some way. But he knew it had to be exhaustion when she climbed in behind the wheel and said, 'That car got a boot, has it?' No one could be attracted to such a prosaic female.

'Have you decided what you're doing?' she asked as they drove back towards the surgery.

He didn't answer so she drove a little further, before adding, 'I don't think you're in any state to drive anywhere at the moment.'

'Well, thank you, Sister Logan!' he replied, but softened the words with a smile. 'Can I prevail upon you to drop me at the bed and breakfast place. I'll walk back and get the car later.'

'Have you any painkillers in your bag?' she asked.

He nodded. 'Can't be much of a drug addict that I didn't think of them this morning, can I?'

'Not much of one,' she admitted. 'Here's the house. There's a bedroom downstairs so you won't have to climb to the next floor.'

James looked at the old red-brick building with the ubiquitous lace curtains at the windows. Pots of geraniums hung from posts along the front verandah and a larger pot was set in an old square frame of iron above the shallow steps.

'Was it a square basketball hoop?' he asked, wanting to sit for a while before he moved again and further aggravated his insistently aching hip.

'This was one of eight hotels along the main street when the gold rush was at its height,' Harriet explained. 'Hotels had to have lights outside to guide the weary traveller. You'll see a similar frame up the road at the last remaining licensed premises.'

James found his interest in the place growing and turned towards his guide and chauffeur.

'Are all the people in town as interested in the past as you are?'

She shrugged, and nodded.

'Now tourists have discovered us, and added a visit to Gold Creek to their tours of the vineyards, we've all boned up on the past, although those of us who grew up here heard the old tales from our cradles.'

Her face was serious, as if she hoped he would respect the history of her village, and he found the serious Sister Logan just as intriguing as the laughing one.

'There doesn't seem to be anyone at home,' he said, gazing towards the house so she wouldn't read that interest in his eyes.

'There is now,' she replied, and sprang nimbly down from the car.

'It's your place?' he asked when she came around and stood ready to catch him if he made a fool of himself and fell over on her doorstep.

'Yes!' She spoke abruptly, her voice deepened by unspoken reservations.

'And you're not overjoyed at having a guest?' he suggested.

'No!' she said, then she sighed. 'But you certainly can't be travelling back over that road today,' she told him. 'Let's get you inside and comfortable and we'll think about the future tomorrow.'

As he forced his aching body up onto the verandah and in through the door she was holding open, her wariness irritated him.

'Whatever happened to country hospitality?' he demanded. 'I thought you bush folk had a tradition of throwing open your doors to wanderers, passing through.'

'You're not passing through,' she said crisply, flinging open a door on the far side of the front parlour and indicating he should enter. 'This used to be the dining room. When it was renovated the old butler's pantry off it was turned into a bathroom. There are towels in that lowboy. If you give me your keys I'll go down and get your suitcase.'

He wanted to protest but the sight of the huge brass bed with its snowy white counterpane and its soft inviting pillows proved his undoing. It was the kind of bed you saw in foreign films, and he could imagine the hero tossing the heroine onto its bouncy softness and the pair of them cavorting among the pillows. Then a stab of pain overcame the erotic fantasy and he handed Harriet his car keys then sank down on the edge of it, bending forward to take off his shoes.

'Here, let me do that,' his bossy nurse said gruffly.

She knelt, and with infinite gentleness eased the shoes off his feet. He looked down at the red-gold curls, bobbing so close to his chest, and wondered if they would feel as soft and silky as they looked.

Rosemary had hated him touching her hair—messing it up, she'd called it. Unless, of course, they'd been in bed—but even then there had been little in the way of caressing. Sex had been just as much a business to Rosemary as the rest of her well-signposted life. Good, of course, but regimented in some way.

'You're exhausted,' Harriet scolded as she straightened. James forgot about Rosemary and imagined Sister Logan bouncing off the pillows. 'Take a couple of painkillers then lie down and rest for a while. Would a massage help?'

He must be less well than he'd thought, he decided. Not only did he have all these fantasies flashing in his head, but the idea of this woman massaging him started a stirring in his groin. He groaned inwardly. She was reluctant to have him in her house as it was. What would she think if he stripped off for a massage and she noticed...?

'I think I'll take your advice and rest a while,' he told her, but he didn't move from where he sat, cross-legged now, on the edge of the bed until she had left the room and shut the door behind her.

CHAPTER FOUR

HARRIET walked slowly out to the kitchen where she put on the kettle, then sat down at the large scrubbed pine table and stared bleakly out the door. She shouldn't have touched James, shouldn't have knelt at his feet to pull off his shoes and thought strange thoughts about where such an action could lead in other circumstances.

Why was this stranger unsettling her so much? Was it just that he was suffering and for as long as she could remember she'd been drawn to creatures who were hurting? Had felt a need to do something to ease their pain?

A shrill whistle interrupted her thoughts and she rose to make a cup of tea. She'd drink it and then go down and get the doctor's car—or maybe she'd just get his suitcase and leave the car where it was. Not that that would fool anyone. It would be all over the village before nightfall that the new doctor was staying at her place.

Something Doug had never done—had never asked to do, in fact, although whether he'd been protecting her reputation or his she was never quite sure.

The tea was hot, burning her lip as she sipped it, and it seemed to have lost its taste, aggravating her instead of refreshing her. She tipped it down the sink and headed for the door. Collecting James Hepworth's car would give her something positive to do.

She set off down the hill towards the surgery, taking a short cut across abandoned properties rather than following the road that wound its way down towards the creek. There was a hint of woodsmoke in the air and the cool breeze brushed her cheek.

She breathed deeply, delighting in the smell, and closed her eyes against the dazzle of the sun as it slipped towards the western hills. Autumn was her favourite time of the year—or at least that's what she thought each autumn when the first fires were lit. Would autumn now bring memories of this stranger?

Her foot struck an old log, half-hidden in the grass, and she was jolted back to reality, but it was a reality with a disturbing new element ruffling the quiet tenor of her days.

The car stood out in front of the old dilapidated building like a bright new toy in a dusty, rough-and-tumble playground. It fitted into the surroundings about as well as James Hepworth would fit into her life, she realised, and felt a sense of sadness overwhelm her. He'd be gone in a month, she reminded herself as she seated herself behind the wheel and gingerly started the engine.

It started with a well-mannered purr but she could feel the harnessed might of the engine and again thought of her unwelcome visitor, wondering what lay hidden beneath his polished façade.

'It's none of your business,' she reminded herself in blunt, no-nonsense tones, and with a sigh that lingered like the woodsmoke in the air around her she released the brake and, before driving the few blocks back to her house, detoured via the hotel where most of the local gossips would be gathered at this time of the day.

'See my fine new car!' she said brightly, taking the two steps in one stride and walking confidently up to the bar. 'I'd like a couple of bottles of mineral water, thanks, Nev. Doug's replacement is recovering from an accident and he's found our one-lane highway a bit hard to take so it looks like I've got me a boarder for a while.'

Which should make things clear before the talk begins, she thought, looking around at the faces of her friends and neighbours while this information sank in.

'Shouldn't think he'd want to take his fancy wheels

back over the road more often than is necessary,' one man remarked.

'He didn't look good to me when I saw him about my hernia this morning,' a woman added. 'Not that I could fault him as a doctor, mind. Real polite and nice he was, and ever so interested in the way it shifts about a bit.'

Harriet hid a smile and wondered what James had made of Rosie's shifting hernia. He'd said nothing slighting or derogatory about any of his patients, which made her think more highly of him. Some of the locums Doug had hired in the past couldn't wait to repeat patients' humorous descriptions of their complaints, a practice which irritated Harriet far more than it amused her.

'Well, it looks like I'm stuck with him for a while,' she told the gathering. 'I'll feed him tonight but you and Betty will have a new dinner customer when my stocks run low, Nev.'

'Will he stay over the weekend, do you think?' someone asked.

'In Gold Creek?' another joked. 'Only if he's mad or got the fever.'

Talk turned to 'the fever', the pursuit of the elusive nuggets of gold that still provided a living for some locals and brought more tourists to the town than the old buildings ever could or would.

'You'll have to bring him to the dance,' Nev reminded Harriet as he handed her the two bottles and her change.

'If he's still here it would be a new experience for him,' she agreed, then she said goodbye and left, her mind boggling at the thought that she might have to entertain James Hepworth over the weekend. Surely not! The road to town wasn't *that* bad!

Returning home, she dropped his suitcase in the living room and tapped lightly on his door. There was no reply so she opened it a crack to peer in and saw him, sleeping. With the lines of strain eased from his face, he looked even more darkly handsome, and she shut the door quickly on both the image and her thoughts.

By the time James appeared at seven-thirty she had dinner prepared and was sitting on the paved area out the back of the house, wondering if she should wake him or let him sleep.

He'd had a shower and his hair was still damp, while his cheeks glowed with the sheen of a fresh shave. He must have found the suitcase she'd left outside his bedroom door for he'd changed from his grey trousers and white shirt to soft shiny chinos and a silky brown T-shirt that did nothing to hide tight muscles in his shoulders and not-too-protuberant abdominal muscles—the beloved 'abs' of the body-builder. Had he been doing weight training as he recuperated?

'Feeling more human?' Harriet asked lightly, trying to dispel a sense of quite illogical happiness.

'Much!' he told her, but little joy was reflected in his eyes which were dark in the soft light shed by the verandah lamps. 'I see you've brought the car up here—or is it down? I seem to have lost my bearings.'

'It's up,' she assured him, then hesitated, uncertain how to suggest that he join her for dinner—wanting to feed him and to look after him, yet not wanting him to feel she was intruding into his life.

She watched him pace around the paved courtyard, like an animal learning new territory through its senses, and felt he approved of her neat backyard with its grapevine, espaliered fruit trees and white wicker furniture.

'Have you always lived here?' he asked, and she chuckled.

'No,' she said. 'One day when we're out on our rounds I'll show you the house where I grew up. I bought this place three years ago. It had been partly renovated by some city people who'd decided they wanted to get away from it all. But Gold Creek proved a bit too far away and they shifted into town. I've been slowly getting it how I want it and my bed and breakfast visitors are helping to pay for the renovations. The downstairs is finished but the upstairs rooms still need a lot of attention.'

'Is that how you spend your off-duty hours?' he asked, stopping his prowling and propping himself against the wall so he could look both at her and the garden.

'Most of them,' she admitted, 'although I still have my grandfather's claim and I do a bit of fossicking now and then.'

James looked as startled as if she'd told him she skinned kangaroos for a hobby.

'Gold fossicking?' he asked.

'Of course,' she said. 'What else at Gold Creek?'

She watched as he assimilated this bit of information—or perhaps rejected it, if the shake of his head was any indication. Then he smiled and her heart jiggled in her chest while her lungs squeezed shut, trapping air she needed desperately.

'And now?' he said. 'I think you mentioned dinner at the hotel. Will you join me there or do I have to eat in solitary splendour?'

Harriet peered suspiciously at him. If he hadn't noticed the aroma of their dinner as he'd walked through the kitchen he must have lost his sense of smell in the accident.

'I've cooked dinner for us,' she muttered, still trying to control the unusual activity in her chest. 'Are you ready to eat?'

'If you're offering some of that delicious stew, I surely am,' he told her, his smile broadening as if he knew exactly what she'd been thinking. 'I only mentioned the hotel to be polite. Actually, I peeked into the pot when I was finding my way around. I haven't smelt anything as good since holidays at Grandma's when I was a kid.'

'Don't overdo the praise,' Harriet told him tartly as

she brushed past him and led the way into the kitchen. 'Anything with onions and a bit of garlic and herbs in it smells great when it's cooking.'

'And here I thought you might appreciate the compliment,' he said mournfully, but she wasn't taken in by his tone. The wretch was teasing her, amusing himself by stirring up emotions she'd rather not be feeling.

It must have been the sleep which had made him more human, she decided a little later as she chuckled at a medical joke she hadn't heard before. And more dangerously attractive as a man!

'So, tell me about Hillview,' he said when they'd finished eating and had pushed their plates aside.

'It's a village much like this,' she said, 'but it was settled later, and because it's closer to town most of the houses have been inhabited since the early days so it doesn't have the neglected, sparsely populated look of Gold Creek. In fact, it's what you might call compact,' she added, smiling as she thought of the way the homes leant upon each other, some being held up by their neighbours while others stood upright thanks to the vines that tangled around them.

'And we do two afternoon sessions there, Tuesday and Thursday?'

Harriet nodded.

'Two lots of three hours. I do a clinic on Fridays as well—see women and babies, do dressings, check on some of the elderly patients. It's the regular influx of tourists here at Gold Creek that warrants the extra sessions. If they're not burning themselves on gas lanterns or spirit stoves, they're falling over old diggings or hurting their backs, panning in the creek. Most weeks we have at least one school party down at the camping grounds and during school holidays the place is packed.'

'How does Doug manage to fit in the sessions here and at Hillview and still practise in town?'

Harriet smiled at him.

'He's hyperactive,' she replied. 'Can't bear it if he's not busy all the time—rushing here and rushing there!' She sighed. Doug's frenetic energy made her tired, just thinking about it. It was one of the reasons she was determined never to give in to his ridiculous notion that they marry. 'He has a partner in town so he only does evenings, Fridays and weekends, but if he's not working he's out at the range, practising or teaching archery to local kids or trying to invent new kinds of feathered tails for his arrows or writing to someone to promote his sport.'

'He does all of that and still finds time for work?' James asked, his eyebrows arching in disbelief.

'And more.' Harriet sighed. 'As I said, he's hyper-active.'

She glanced across the table as she finished speaking to find her colleague's eyes fixed on her. His scrutiny brought back the discomfort she'd felt earlier, spoiling her pleasant post-meal lethargy.

'You don't seem too enamoured of his sport,' James said, and Harriet shook her head.

'It's very boring for the onlookers,' she admitted, 'and it seems so pointless. But Pop always said that all sport was pointless to those not involved. He said it was like life—you had to be a participant not an onlooker to really get the most out of it.'

She felt the sudden sweep of sadness that thinking of Pop always produced, and stood up hurriedly, carrying their plates across to the sink.

James watched her go, puzzling over the contradictions he saw in this woman—so organised, efficient and in control one minute, then suddenly philosophical. She'd been saddened by her thoughts, he realised, a sheen of tears turning her eyes a darker blue.

He pushed himself to his feet, wanting to be closer to her, to get to know her better—the soft vulnerable Harriet, not the bossy nurse.

'I'll help,' he offered, and reached for the teatowel she had slung over one shoulder.

'No you won't,' she snapped, grabbing it out of his hand. 'Normally, you'd be doing the lot because I believe in a fair division of labour, but you're obviously not as well as you think you are and I need you here—as a doctor of course—' she knew the words were coming out all wrong but she kept going '—so I'd prefer it if you rested. There's a cabinet full of books in the living room and comfortable chairs with foot-rests. Take yourself off in there and I'll bring some coffee shortly.'

She turned from the sink as she finished this list of instructions and added, 'Or would you prefer tea in the evening?'

James tried to answer her, to say coffee would be fine, but there was a smudge of moisture on her cheek and the sparkle of a tear trapped in her dark lashes, and all he could do was stare at her and wonder what pain she hid behind her brisk but caring exterior and why he should be affected by this woman's hidden distress.

'Who was Pop?' he asked, and she turned away, bending over the sink and scrubbing furiously at a battered saucepan.

He hesitated for a moment then realised he wasn't going to get an answer. She'd shut him off—out of her thoughts—as effectively as if she'd locked a door between them.

'Coffee will be fine,' he said as he limped away.

Harriet heard him go and forced the tense muscles in her neck and shoulders to relax. The people who said time healed all wounds had no idea what they were talking about. It had been six years since Pop died and still his memory had the power to sneak up and stab her in the heart when she was least expecting it.

Harriet finished the dishes, made a pot of coffee, set a cup and saucer, some biscuits a patient had given her and a tiny jug of cream on a tray and carried it through to the living room.

'Not joining me?' he asked as she set the tray on a small table by his chair.

'No, I want to go back down to the surgery,' she said. 'I've some filing to do and I want to check the appointments for the morning. Marj helps out with the reception work but she finds it hard to say no to people so we often end up with a morning list that will take all day to get through, which is OK on Mondays and Wednesdays but doesn't work when we do Hillview in the afternoon.'

She rushed through this explanation, made uneasy by the way he was looking at her. For some reason her own words, 'finds it hard to say no' kept running through her head like an insistent line of a song that refused to go away.

'I'll see you later,' she finished feebly, hoping he'd be well and truly asleep in her downstairs bedroom by the time she returned.

But escape was not to be so easy.

'What do you do with the patients if Marj has overbooked?' he asked.

'I phone the ones I think aren't urgent and ask them to come Wednesday or I ring Doug and tell him he'll have to get out here an hour earlier to fit them all in.'

He smiled at her and she felt a quiver of response start in her toes. She refused to let it go further than her knees, quelling it as he said, 'Well, at least I'll be on hand for an early start. Six perhaps, or seven?'

'It won't be that early,' she told him without an answering smile. 'Do you want me to tap on your door and wake you? Let you know, say, half an hour before breakfast is ready?'

Would half an hour be enough time for him to shower and shave and do whatever other little rituals he did each morning? The intimacy of considering his morning ritu-

als made the quiver creep higher but she blocked it out
of her mind with another question.

'And do you like a cooked breakfast or are you a toast
and coffee man?'

'Harriet!'

He said the word so sternly she stopped thinking of
more questions to ask and looked directly at him, surprised to see the depth of understanding in his eyes.

'I know my being here is upsetting you and I want
you to know how much I appreciate it. But I refuse to
be more of a nuisance than I have to be. I can wake
myself up, I can make my own coffee and toast—'

'But this is a bed and breakfast,' she protested. 'Your
board includes breakfast—you shouldn't have to get it
yourself.'

'And did it include dinner tonight?' James asked
gently. 'Wasn't that offered to me as a guest in your
house rather than as a boarder?'

Harriet knew she was blushing because her skin flared
with heat, but she said the words she knew must be
said—right now—at once—before anyone, herself in
particular, got any ideas about anything!

'No, you're a boarder,' she said firmly. 'And as you're
here on a longer-term basis, at least during the week, I'll
do your dinner and lunch as well. I cut sandwiches and
cook for myself so it's no hassle. I'll work out how much
to charge you and let you know, and now I've got to
go.'

She hurried from the room before he could argue, and
before the quiver became so strong he'd be able to see
it from where he sat.

What to charge him was the least of her problems.
Right now Harriet had to cope with the disturbing sensations she was experiencing whenever she was near
him. She had to figure out why she was reacting as she
was and how she was going to prevent it happening as

they worked and ate—and, no, not slept—together for the next four weeks.

'At least I should have the weekends free,' she muttered to a cow that was grazing on the spare allotment near the surgery. 'Time off for good behaviour!'

But it was not to be! By the time Friday came it was evident that the four days' work had overtaxed her locum's strength. Pain had painted the greyness back in his skin and lurked behind the angry darkness in his eyes.

'Stupid, useless old crock,' she heard him berating himself on Friday morning as she started the coffee and made some pancakes for their breakfast.

'Stay in bed and rest,' she called through the wall. 'I'll bring your breakfast in then I'm off to Hillview and you can have the whole day to yourself.'

But the muttering continued and James hobbled out into the kitchen and slumped into a chair.

'I will not stay in bed,' he said, squeezing the words out from between tight lips. 'I spent three bloody months in bed and swore I'd never lie down in the daytime ever again.'

'Well, bully for you,' Harriet countered, trying to ignore how attractive he looked in his pale trousers and soft chocolate brown sweater. 'You couldn't possibly go back on such a decision for the sake of common sense, now could you?'

She'd hoped to make him smile, although she knew the danger of that expression, but all she got was an angry scowl and the enquiry, 'Isn't that coffee ready yet?'

'You drink too much coffee,' she told him, leaning across the table to slide a plate in front of him. 'That's probably what makes you so bad-tempered.'

Reaching into the oven, she brought out a serving

dish, piled high with golden pancakes, and set them down on the table in front of him.

'Coffee will be two minutes,' she added, bending down to the oven again to retrieve a plate of crisply fried bacon. She pushed this across the table towards him and waved her hand towards the dishes and jars already assembled. 'Maple syrup, rum and maple syrup, butter and cream,' she said. 'I thought we might give our cholesterol another day off.'

Easing the plunger gently through the coffee, she sniffed appreciatively at the aroma and carried the pot to the table.

'Help yourself! Enjoy!' she offered, then she waited to see how he'd respond.

'Did you guess I was going to wake up in a foul mood and cook all this up to soothe the wounded beast?' he asked, no smile glimmering but with a definite lightening of his features.

She tried a smile of her own.

'Actually, I usually treat myself to this on Saturday mornings but decided I'd better go to town and do some shopping tomorrow so I'd have my special feast today.'

'Thank you,' he said, reaching out to take some pancakes and adding strips of bacon to his plate.

What for? she'd have liked to ask, but didn't because she didn't want him thanking her for breakfast. She'd rather think he was thanking her for caring about his welfare, although the way she'd bullied him and ordered him around all week was hardly likely to have produced gratitude.

'It was for your own good,' she said, then saw his startled look as the words diverted him from his breakfast. 'I'm sorry, I was thinking aloud,' she added. 'Thinking how well I fitted your description of bossy.'

'But only ever for my own good,' he repeated gravely, then he smiled. 'I've never prescribed it but pancakes and bacon have made me feel considerably better. With your aversion to drug-addicted doctors in mind I've been trying to keep off the painkillers so I didn't sleep much last night.'

'That's ridiculous,' Harriet told him, trying desperately to ignore the effects of the smile. 'The occasional analgesic isn't going to qualify you for immediate drug addiction.'

'No,' he agreed in a more serious voice, 'but with a free day ahead of me I thought I'd experiment to see how bad things still were without the relief of analgesics.'

Harriet studied him, seeing the paleness still lingering in his cheeks and the dark shadows under his eyes.

'Pretty bad, huh?' she said, sympathy for him tugging at her heart.

'Pretty bad,' he agreed, but his smile widened and he seemed about to add a rider when the phone rang.

James watched Harriet answer it, wondering if he was imagining her relief at the interruption. She was one of the most natural, uncomplicated people he'd ever met, yet he'd noticed that she shied away from him if ever their casual conversation turned personal.

She was saying yes and no quite calmly but he could see her fingers tightening on the receiver and wondered if the call was bad news.

'Trouble?' he asked as she hung up.

'You could say that,' she said, a wry smile twisting her lips. 'Some idiot down at the camping ground has stabbed his mate. Says it was an accident, they were just fooling around.' She frowned and checked her watch. 'His voice sounded odd. If it wasn't seven-thirty in the morning I'd say he was drunk. I've got to go. I'll patch him up and go straight on to Hillview. Will you find yourself some lunch?'

James eased himself upright and found that his hip was weight-bearing far more happily since he'd been sitting instead of lying down.

'There's no rule to say you can't be drunk at seven-thirty in the morning,' he told her. 'And you're not going off to deal with some knife-wielding drunk on your own.'

'Well, you're not coming with me,' Harriet retorted. 'You need to rest your leg.'

She ran a hand through her curls, leaving them springing up more defiantly than ever. 'What's more, I go off and deal with accidents all the time. I don't need a back-up.'

She snagged her bag off the chair near the phone and headed for the front door.

'I don't care what you're used to doing on your own,' James growled, hurrying as fast as he could after her. 'Today you're taking me with you or I'll *walk* down to the camping ground and think what that will do for my injuries.'

He reached the battered old Jeep as she started the engine, and hauled himself painfully into his usual spot in the passenger seat. After home visits and two return trips to Hillview he was coming to know the vehicle's idiosyncrasies and was even beginning to believe Harriet's claim about its springs.

She refused to acknowledge his presence, staring ahead with quite unnecessary concentration as the road was too narrow for speed and the only traffic they ever seemed to pass were the wandering cows.

'I haven't been down here before,' he said as she swung the car left along a rocky, untarred track. 'I've seen the tops of the tents from the back of the surgery but had no idea how to get here.'

She relented enough to glance his way.

'It was sited where the creek-bank is high enough for the ground not to flood if there's a cloudburst in the hills,' she said crisply. 'There was a farmer's cottage here originally and the old trees he planted provide shade for the campers. There are usually a dozen or so tents here most days, and up to fifty during the school holidays.'

Turning left again, they crossed a cattle grid obviously intended to keep the cattle out—not the campers in—and pulled up beside a neat brick amenities block.

'His mate said they'd wait here,' she said, her voice suddenly doubtful as she searched for a sign of the injured man.

James was glad he'd come, and suspected she was, too. Not many women would feel happy about walking into the male section of a public toilet. He watched her turn off the engine then scramble out of the car, her fears hidden behind her determined façade. He climbed down too quickly and had to steady himself against the cab until he'd regained his balance.

'Are you there, Cliff?' Harriet called. 'I'm the local nurse and I'm here to look at your friend's wound.'

'We're in here,' a gruff voice answered. 'He's real crook so I brought him in here so he could be sick in peace.'

As she headed towards the door an unfamiliar presentiment tickled along James's nerves. He shot out a hand and stopped her.

'I'll go in there,' he said, seizing the bag and shouldering her almost roughly out of his way. 'You wait here.'

'I'll come with you,' she protested, and he turned towards her, a black anger churning inside him.

'You will do precisely as you're told,' he commanded. 'You'll take orders for once, instead of giving them, and if I call out and tell you to get in the car and start the engine you'll do that, too—understand?'

She nodded, but he guessed that while she would probably wait outside for a second or two—sheer shock at being ordered around might keep her immobile—she had no intention of turning tail and leaving him to face the unknown alone. The thought both cheered and infuriated him but there was no time to sort out which emotion was dominant.

He walked into the shadowy gloom of the urinal and was immediately assailed by a variety of emotions. Most immediate was relief that he'd insisted Harriet stay outside, while another part of his brain was asking why on earth he'd accepted this job—so far removed from the pristine surroundings and ordered, sterile atmosphere of an operating theatre that it was like another world. Then fury mounted high enough to wipe away all extraneous thoughts. That these louts would play a trick like this on Harriet—on any woman!

He drew himself up to his full six feet one and said in icy tones, 'I gather from the blood you've splattered around this place that your friend is really injured. When you've dressed him and yourself bring him outside and I'll look at his wound.'

'But it's bad,' the man who lay on the floor whined.

'You'll live long enough to pull some trousers on unless you've picked up so much infection, playing around in here, that a tetanus shot's too late.'

It was a cheap trick but it galvanised the man into action.

'It wasn't my idea,' he protested, climbing unsteadily to his feet and pulling on a pair of filthy shorts. 'And I wrapped my shirt around my arm so it wouldn't get dirty.'

James shuddered as he considered the micro-organisms and bacteria likely to be lurking in the man's shirt.

'Come outside where I can see properly and we'll take a look,' he relented, and turned just in time to prevent Harriet from bursting through the door.

'You should have told me you were all right,' she scolded, catching hold of his arm as if to reassure herself that he was whole.

'I'm fine,' he said gently. 'Now, how about you get

out some antiseptic solution and we take a look at this fellow's wound.'

She dropped her hand from him immediately and moved across to the wide stainless-steel sink where she'd set out the things they might need. He smiled at the sight of the silver kidney dish she always carried. It was as old-fashioned as medicine itself—but still had its uses.

'Sit here,' he told the patient, recognising one of the folding chairs Harriet kept in the back of the Jeep. She couldn't have been as worried as he'd imagined to have prepared so well for this impromptu surgery. 'Let's take a look,' he said, switching his mind from Harriet to work.

'Lovely sterile dressing,' she muttered as she peeled away the shirt and passed him a swab doused in antiseptic. 'We'd probably do better pouring solution over his arm.'

She had stepped closer and was peering over his shoulder, a position which with anyone else would have aggravated him, but the contours of her body, the warm, syrupy smell of her breath...

The cut was a long slash, stretching from the fleshy part of the forearm almost to the wrist. James could see the debris scattered through it and agreed with Harriet that a thorough dousing of the area should be the first move.

'Could you mix up some solution for me to flood it?' he asked, turning and inadvertently brushing against her soft, full breast.

'Right away,' she said blithely, but he noticed her skin had coloured and she moved very quickly out of his orbit.

'I think you should go into town and have this seen to at the hospital,' he told the patient.

'This little gash?' the young man scoffed. 'What do you think I am, a sissy? Just stitch it up, it'll be right!'

Resisting an urge to hit him on the head with something blunt and heavy, James said, 'Unfortunately, it's not the kind of wound I can just stitch up. I think it should be left open in case there's an infection already forming there, and we don't have the necessary petrolatum gauze and fluffed material to dress the wound so it can be treated for the infection, before closing it.'

He ignored the wild signals of Harriet's eyebrows, knowing full well that she was telling him they did, indeed, have the required dressings at the surgery. He knew because he'd made it his business to check what was in stock, but he wanted this youth and his mate out of the town, not tripping up to the surgery every day to ogle Harriet and make a nuisance of themselves while she changed the dressings.

'I'll do what I can to clean it out. How long since you had a tetanus shot?'

The man shivered as if the thought of an injection was painful then admitted, 'Had one last year when I came off my bike and got a few grazes.'

He indicated his leg where the scar tissue was still new enough to be pink and shiny.

'On track to self-destruct, are you?' James asked him, and was surprised when the young man shrugged.

'No one much to care if I did,' he mumbled. He nodded to his companion who was emerging sheepishly from the darkness. ''Cept me mate,' he added.

'The same mate who plunged a knife into you?' Harriet asked, and James felt his patient shudder.

'We were fooling around,' he protested. 'It was my fault as much as his.'

'OK. Let's clean you up and see what's what,' James told him, stirred by an unexpected sympathy for this crude and grubby youth.

He turned to Harriet. 'Solution please, Sister,' he said crisply, but he saw a similar emotion reflected in her eyes and wanted to hold her for a moment and remind her that they couldn't change the world. All they could do was help ill or hurting folk who ventured into their little part of it.

Then he imagined Sister Logan's reaction to being held in his arms and decided he'd better stick to the more practical aspects of medicine.

CHAPTER FIVE

HARRIET watched James's hands manoeuvre the tweezers as he probed the wound, removing the more obvious pieces of foreign matter. She could imagine him as a surgeon, his precise movements making the delicate incisions cleanly, his deft fingers tackling the most intricate microscopic work with neat precision.

'There's no apparent nerve or ligament damage and no major blood vessels involved so I'm going to wrap it up and send you to town—'

'No, Doc, stitch it up,' the patient pleaded. 'We'll leave and won't come back to bug you or the nurse.'

Harriet was surprised by the panic in the young man's voice. Had they been in trouble in town? She tried to think if she'd heard of any recent incidents, only half listening as James explained to their patient that if he closed the wound with a piece of foreign matter still inside it could become badly infected.

'We'll get it checked by a doctor in the next place we stop,' his mate promised. 'We're heading north.'

She could feel James hesitating and wondered why. Surely he couldn't care what happened to this stranger? She felt concerned for the young man but, then, she always worried about people who seemed to have no roots. Her own were so firmly embedded in the rocky gullies around Gold Creek that she couldn't imagine not having somewhere to call home.

'Come up to the surgery and I'll stitch you up, then,' James said at last. 'And I'll give you some antibiotics which might help prevent an infection, but be sure you take them all.'

Harriet sensed the relief in the pair and she forgot about feeling sorry for them as her suspicions sharpened once again.

'I'll tape an antiseptic dressing over it until you get up there,' James continued, and turned to Harriet who had one ready to hand him. 'Can you drop me back at the surgery?'

She nodded, knowing he was aware she should be on her way to Hillview by now. She watched him tape the dressing into place, her mind racing. There was no way she was going to leave him alone with these two dubious characters. He was a tall man and his muscles were well defined—too well defined for her peace of mind at times—but he was also convalescent and no match for two younger men if things turned nasty.

'Do you know where to go?' she asked the visitors, and felt slightly better when they both shook their heads. It meant they hadn't already checked out the place as part of some devious plan. 'You'd better follow me,' she told them.

Snapping her bag shut, she headed for the Jeep. James walked directly—and closely—behind her and she had the strangest feeling, almost as if she was enjoying his protective attitude. Then she shrugged it off. It was common sense for the two of them to stay together—especially if he had the same uneasiness about their behaviour and motives.

'You go on to Hillview. I'll walk back up to the house when I've fixed his arm,' James said as she pulled into her usual parking place beside the surgery.

'No way,' she argued. 'I'm not leaving you with those two desperadoes.'

He turned towards her.

'I don't think they're as bad as they look,' he said, a slight frown puckering his brow. 'I know they pulled a silly stunt down there, and that they're very unappealing-looking specimens of the human race, but there's something admirable in their mateship...'

His voice trailed away and he looked beyond her to where the pair were approaching on a large and noisy motorbike.

'I haven't come across anyone like them since my stints in A and E or Cas, back when I was training.'

He eased himself out of the seat, setting his uninjured leg on the ground first. Harriet waited, holding her breath as she usually did until he'd found his balance and begun to move away. He was affected by the two young men, she could tell that, affected enough to have set aside his exhaustion and pain. But why?

She slipped out and overtook him, going on ahead to unlock the doors.

'Won't your patients be waiting for you?' James asked, coming up behind her at the cupboard and watching as she sorted through sutures to find what she needed. 'I'll be quite safe here on my own.'

So he didn't care for support! Well, he'd done the same for her, insisting he walked into that amenities block at the camping reserve.

'I'm staying,' she told him firmly. 'And my patients won't be waiting. Didn't anything strike you at Hillview?' She stood aside so he could choose the local anaesthetic he wanted from the refrigerator.

'Strike me?' His eyebrows lifted and he gave her a puzzled look.

'No patients waiting when we first arrived, even though we were late both days?'

He shook his head.

'You're right, there weren't any, but they soon flocked in once we'd unlocked the door and opened all the windows.'

Harriet smiled at him.

'They see us driving down the hill into town,' she explained. 'And probably hear the old wreck of a vehicle. No one leaves home until they know we're almost there because they realise how unpredictable our lives can be. Today's a well-woman and baby clinic so there's no great rush to get there. The women will turn up when it suits them anyway. They fit me in between feeds or housework.'

James matched her smile with a fever-inducing one of his own.

'It's very reassuring to discover medicine like this still exists. Most GP work these days is regimented by all those time and motion studies on efficient practice, while this seems more adapted to suit the local conditions.' His eyes looked into hers and he added in a softer voice, 'Of course, I realise it's the people involved who make it work, special people—'

'Are you there, Doc?' a loud voice interrupted, and Harriet felt a sharp stab of disappointment as James turned abruptly away from her to answer the summons.

She walked after him, carrying the small tray with sutures, swabs and dressings.

'Are you going north, looking for jobs?' James was asking the patient as he inserted the local.

The youth shrugged and his mate replied, 'Thought we might try to find his old man. His dad shot through years ago but he's supposed to be some big building contractor in North Queensland and we've both got experience as labourers.'

'I hope you find him,' Harriet heard herself saying, passing a swab and watching James work, although her mind had moved back swiftly to a past she'd tried to forget. 'When you do, try to put the past behind you and meet him adult to adult. If you hang onto bitterness it's like putting up a great wall of emotion between you and him and you won't make proper contact through it.'

All three turned to look at her and she realised how adamantly she must have spoken. Still, it was good advice, learned from her own experience.

James switched his attention back to his patient and the mate hovered over the pair of them, but the silence in the room demanded something she didn't want to give—demanded further explanation, personal revelations to reinforce her words.

'My mum took off too,' she said as lightly as she could, handing the first suture to James, 'and I went looking for her when I finished school. I didn't know how angry I was with her until we met and I let all this awful stuff come pouring out. Accusations, recriminations, rage, hate and general adolescent self-pity—so much garbage dumped all at once on the poor woman it's a wonder she didn't take off again.'

She could feel James's surprise in the stillness of his body, but she wanted these two young men to understand how badly things could go if they didn't approach the possible meeting in as unemotional a way as possible.

'I don't blame my dad,' the patient said, turning to look at Harriet while James stitched. 'He was only my age, nineteen, when they got married and my mum was pregnant with my sister, then I came along and he was twenty-one, with two kids squawling around the house…'

Harriet nodded, feeling sympathy for the two young people who'd been trapped by their hormones and the boundless optimism of youth. James drew the final suture through the skin and tied it off then puffed antiseptic powder around the wound, before reaching for a dressing.

'I'd better take some details for a patient card,' she said, and motioned the mate to follow her out to the reception area. 'Make sure he sees a doctor if it becomes at all angry and inflamed-looking,' she said.

'You don't think I want him getting any worse hurt, do you?' the young man asked belligerently, and Harriet smiled.

'No, I don't,' she said gently. 'And, in spite of the fact you managed to stab him, I believe you do care about him. Friendship is a very special thing so hang onto it.'

'What happened to your mum?' the big lout with the unexpectedly soft heart asked.

Harriet dredged up her most cheerful smile and lied to this man she would probably never see again.

'Oh, she and I are great friends now!'

She glanced past him to see James emerge from his room. One look at his face told her that he'd heard her words, and she didn't need a second look to tell her he disbelieved them.

She filled out the card, had the injured man sign a Medicare slip and moved swiftly away from James towards the back of the house where she retrieved her bag and keys.

'I'll be off now,' she said as she headed for the door. 'Do you want me to drop you back at the house?'

'No, I'll walk back later,' he replied. 'I thought I might stay a while and read through some patient files.'

She was about to brush past him when he detained her with the lightest of touches on her arm.

'Harriet,' he began, his eyes full of questions.

'I'm already very late,' she said, and moved away, already regretting the revelations she'd made in this man's hearing.

There was a lot to be said for Doug's frenetic pursuit of his work and his hobbies, she decided as she drove the familiar road to Hillview. At least they consumed him to the exclusion of all else so it would never have occurred to Doug to wonder about her childhood or question why she'd been brought up by an elderly grandfather.

The clinic was uneventful but Harriet was sorry when the last patient had been seen and the final visit made.

She usually looked forward to returning home on Fridays, relishing the thought of two whole days free from anything but emergency calls. But tonight meant going home to her unwanted boarder, to a resumption of the irritating physical symptoms she was still experiencing in his presence.

In fact, even thinking about him produced a shivery sensation in her spine and an unsettled feeling in the region of her stomach.

She drove more slowly than usual over the rough dirt road, watching the early dusk begin to settle over the area. The road beneath the cypress pines was dark and gloomy, matching her mood so precisely she was surprised when she came out and found the colours of the sunset still striping the sky with red and petal pink and a dusky orange.

As she approached the house she could see lamplight, glowing behind the curtains. The treacherous thought that it was nice to have someone to welcome her home was immediately denied, but when she walked in and saw the signs of dinner being prepared in the kitchen and found an icy drink and a plate of biscuits and cheese waiting for her on the outside table it resurfaced, filling her with such pleasure that she greeted James with a delighted smile.

'You'll spoil me if you keep doing things like this,' she warned him.

'Perhaps you deserve a bit of spoiling,' he told her, waving her to a chair and turning his attention back to her kettle barbecue.

'What have you got in there that smells so delicious?' she asked, picking up the drink and sipping at it.

'Roast leg of lamb. I didn't dare try to work your oven but I've a barbecue like this at home so I understand them. Successful day?'

It was too perfectly 'house and garden' to be true, she realised, chuckling at her thought.

'Yes, the day was fine, just long,' she conceded. 'In fact, so long that I was going to send you up to the pub for dinner and make do with a piece of toast myself.' Then she realised what he'd said earlier. 'Where on earth did you get a leg of lamb? And those were new potatoes I saw in the kitchen. Where did they come from? You haven't been to town, have you, jolting over that road again?'

A deep laugh rumbled up from somewhere in his chest—the first real laugh she'd heard from him.

'No, I haven't been to town but only because I'm scared if I drive once more over that road I might never force myself to come back.'

His smile made his eyes more golden, she decided, a tawny gold like a lion's mane. When he began to speak again she had to remind herself to concentrate on his words not his eyes.

'I decided to drop in and visit Mrs Reynolds and found her grandson had just arrived—a spritely young-ster of about seventy, he was. He'd brought in the best part of a butchered lamb from his property and they pressed the leg on me, telling me you didn't look after yourself properly and how good it was that I was staying with you because that meant you had to cook proper meals. Then Janet went out and dug some potatoes and also produced a lettuce and tomatoes for a salad. She even supplied the rosemary.'

Harriet thought some very uncomplimentary things about her friends, talking to the new doctor this way, but all she said was, 'Well, I'd better go up and wash a few layers of dust off before you're ready to serve the masterpiece.'

She hurried away, the domesticity of the little scene unnerving her.

Refreshed by her shower, she was then faced by a choice of clothing. With the nights getting cooler, she would

have opted for a moth-eaten old tracksuit as suitable at-
tire for a Friday night at home, but the effort James had
taken over dinner and the table set beneath the lamps in
the garden called for a little more effort than that.

She searched through her wardrobe and finally settled
on a pair of dark blue velvet lounging pyjamas her friend
Elly had given her last Christmas.

'You haven't one glamorous article of clothing in
your entire wardrobe,' Elly had complained. 'Every
woman needs something nice to slip into occasionally.
And you certainly need something special to stir that
slowcoach Doug into action.'

Harriet had protested over this disparagement of Doug
but had accepted the gift with a tingle of excitement, as
if the mere thought of wearing the pyjamas to please a
man had affected her.

Yet when she'd eased into the slim-fitting pants and
had pulled the tunic top over her head she frowned at
her reflection. True, they were definitely wear-at-home
clothes, and they covered every inch of skin so could
hardly be called sexy, but they did something to her eyes
that bothered her, and the velvet felt so soft she wanted
to stroke it. Or wanted someone else to stroke it!

The thought brought colour flaring to her cheeks and
she had just decided to change into something less—
different—when James called from the bottom of the
steps.

She dabbed a touch of pink gloss on her lips, grimaced
at her unfamiliar self, then went quickly down the stairs
as if she wore a velvet lounging suit for dinner every
evening. And she might have, for all the notice he took
of it.

'I've some iced soup for starters,' he explained as she
walked into the kitchen, 'and the lamb is about done.
I'm OK with the cooking part of meal preparation,' he
added, 'but it's timing it all so it's ready to serve when

I'm ready to eat that still gets to me. I tend to get a bit panicky.'

Panicky? James? Harriet stared at him. She hadn't been surprised to find he could cook a meal—most men could these days—but to admit to being less than perfect in the presentation of it?

'I'm sure you'll get it right with practice,' she replied, and saw a swift grin flash across his face.

'I'm hoping I won't have to practise for much longer,' he admitted, ushering her out to the courtyard and pulling a chair out from the table for her. 'My mother forced me into it as therapy when I first came out of hospital and had to go home so someone could keep an eye on me. She said if I had to do some standing and walking each day I should at least make myself useful.'

Harriet found herself laughing, her doubts about her pyjamas forgotten.

'Sounds like a sensible woman, your mother,' she said. 'What does she do?'

It was nothing more than politeness, but even in the lamplight, Harriet saw his eyes soften.

'She's an artist,' he said quietly, and the words were underlined with a kind of love that pressed on the bruised part inside Harriet where her mother's memory resided. 'She paints still life, flowers and fruit mostly but with deep rich colours that wrap around you and make you feel good.'

'I hope you tell her that,' Harriet murmured. She picked up her glass and took a deep draught of the cold soda, but he must have noticed something because he touched her gently on the shoulder and said, 'Your mother's dead, isn't she?'

'I don't want to talk about it,' Harriet told him, shaking off his sympathy with his hand. 'Where's this soup? I'm starving.'

He said no more, simply disappearing into the kitchen

and returning a short time later with two bowls of pale green liquid, each decorated with a tiny sprig of mint.

'Cold pea and lettuce,' he told her. 'It was my one claim to fame in the culinary department before my mother took me in hand. You had frozen peas in the freezer and I used the outer leaves of Janet's lettuce.'

Had James sensed her withdrawal and was he now using this harmless babble about soup recipes to give her time to recover her equilibrium? She hoped not, but as she stirred and then tasted the soup she was glad of the respite.

'That was delicious,' she told him some hours later, when the meal was finished and the plates removed to the kitchen. He had brought out coffee and they sat, the relaxed feeling of repletion keeping them from even thinking about the dishes. 'Your mother taught you well.'

He smiled, but she saw the sudden alertness in his eyes and was sorry she'd mentioned mothers.

'You told those lads about your mother this morning so why is it so hard to talk to me about it?' he asked, his voice deep and low, as if her answer might mean something to him.

'I thought they needed to know how difficult the actual contact with a long-lost parent can be,' she told him calmly. 'It might prepare them for what lies ahead.'

'And because they're warned they might do it better than you did?'

She shrugged.

'It's not important what I did,' she said. 'No one can undo the past.'

He reached forward and took her hand, holding it in one of his and stroking the velvet of her suit with the other—up and down her arm, like someone absent-mindedly stroking a cat.

'No, but you can talk about it and maybe see it in

another perspective so the memory no longer has the power to haunt you.'

She snatched her hand from his and glared at him. 'Don't psychoanalyse me, James Hepworth,' she raged. 'If you want to practise that branch of medicine try some on yourself and face up to a future that may not include surgery, instead of brooding over the past as if it had been your only real chance at happiness.'

'Brooding?' he demanded, with a fine glare of his own. 'I'm not brooding!'

'Well, you're giving a damn good imitation of it,' Harriet retorted. She pushed back the chair and stood, and the anger drained out of her as suddenly as the saw-dust from an old toy, leaving her feeling cold and deflated.

'I shouldn't be yelling at you when you've just cooked me a wonderful dinner,' she mumbled. 'Would you like more coffee?'

He grinned and shook his head.

'For a redhead, you're not too good at sustaining your temper, are you?'

She shrugged. 'Not too good,' she admitted. 'It flares up and then it's gone, especially in a case like this when I had no right to criticise you in the first place.'

She headed for the kitchen and ran water into the sink but there was no escape because he followed, refuting her words.

'That's rubbish, Harriet. We're working together, living together! If you can't say what you're thinking it will be most uncomfortable for both of us. Do you really think I'm brooding?'

Her stomach clenched and her heart did the weird thing it did every morning when she saw him for the first time in the day. But he'd asked the question and she was going to answer it.

'I think you're unhappy over something that goes deeper than the accident,' she admitted. 'I know your injuries have thrown your career plans into turmoil, but a little setback like that shouldn't cause the deep-down misery that seems to follow you around.'

She sloshed the detergent into the water and began on the glassware, pretending to concentrate on getting each item clean.

'A little setback?' James growled, moving closer so she could feel the heat of his body along her spine. 'You call an accident that puts someone in hospital for months then convalescing for several more a little setback?'

He wasn't questioning the deep-down misery bit, Harriet realised, stacking the glasses on the draining-board.

'Well, that's all it is,' she assured him. 'Once you're well again things will seem so much better. This period of relative inactivity is giving you time to consider other options. And this particular period should be reminding you that patients are people, not just bits of abdomen or liver tissue.'

'It's certainly doing that,' he said, and his mood must have shifted as quickly as hers had for the words were deep, with husky undertones that pressed on Harriet's backbone and made her shiver as she slid the plates into the water and rubbed the mop over the first of them.

It was the false togetherness that eating with him had imposed, Harriet decided. It made her feel edgy and uncomfortable. But not as edgy and uncomfortable as having him wipe the dishes while she washed, his fingers accidentally brushing against hers from time to time, his fresh man-smell invading her nostrils, his presence sending every tiny cell in her body into an almost electric awareness of him.

'Are you fit enough to make the journey back to Sydney tomorrow?' she asked when an accidental brush of skin on skin sent her taut nerves twanging.

'Trying to get rid of me, Harriet?' Before she realised

what he was doing James had put his hands on her shoulders and had turned her to face him.

She tried to avoid the dark eyes, looking so questioningly down at her, but his gaze caught hers—and held it—brown eyes clashing with blue.

'I wonder why?' he added, almost under his breath, while his head dipped forward—closer and closer—until his face went out of focus and his lips brushed hers, burning a path across them before returning to cool them with a long, gentle, but definitely exploratory kiss.

'Why did you do that?' she demanded when she'd detached herself with difficulty from his grasp and was resting back against the sink.

He ran his fingers through his hair, unsettling the usually immaculate neatness.

'I don't know,' he admitted with a candid grin. 'Could we put it down to momentary madness? Or perhaps to the fact that I love the feel of velvet and I've been wanting to run my hands over you ever since you first appeared in that suit.'

'Huh!' Harriet snorted. 'I don't think much of either excuse, and the only thing you're going to run your hands over is a teatowel and the rest of those dishes.'

She silently congratulated herself on having handled the situation so calmly but she knew if she left the support of the sink her legs would buckle under her and she would make a complete and utter fool of herself.

However, if she didn't leave the support of the sink she'd have to stand here beside him while he finished wiping the dishes.

'I'll finish those!' she said abruptly, and tried to twitch the teatowel out of his hand, but his fingers tangled in it and held, drawing her closer—away from her reliable prop.

'I won't run my hands over you,' he promised. 'Not right here and now. And not because I think you don't want me to, Harriet Logan. You didn't have to kiss me back, now did you?'

She shook her head, her entire body bending to some force this man imposed.

'I won't do it because I don't think the time is right, and because you're quite correct about some "deep-down misery", as you called it.'

He bent his head and repeated that gentle touch of his lips to hers before he added, 'But don't think I'm not attracted to you because I am. I'm just not certain that giving in to this attraction would be a good thing for either of us.'

Yet he kissed her once again in spite of his words, a kiss that seared its way along nerves and skin and sinew, waking every atom in her body to a vibrancy that made her shiver with delight. Her lips parted beneath his tender assault and her body edged closer, fitting itself to his as if they were two parts of a whole.

They broke apart minutes, or possibly hours, later and Harriet raised her fingers to her lips and touched them to make sure she hadn't imagined the sensations. He pressed his forefinger against her wrist, then touched her cheek, her nose and eyebrow, all the time his eyes holding hers, transmitting messages of desire she couldn't mistake.

'Perhaps I should go back to Sydney, whether I'm up to it or not,' he said gruffly, answering a question he hadn't answered earlier. 'Unless there's a nunnery somewhere close by that would lock you up for the weekend.'

CHAPTER SIX

HARRIET had expected to sleep badly, her body too restless to relax, yet she'd drifted off almost as soon as she'd settled into her bed and hadn't woken until the bird chorus began next morning. When the implications of James Hepworth's strange conversation finally struck her!

She snuggled under the bedclothes and thought about attraction, and found that even thinking of it produced peculiar sensations in her body. Thank goodness she hadn't agreed with him when he'd talked about wanting to run his hands over her—hadn't admitted that her body was reacting to his in an unpredictable fashion. At least now she could deny it—pretend it wasn't happening.

Which means, she told herself, pushing back the covers and shivering in the cool morning air, you'll have to stop kissing him back!

Maybe he won't kiss me again, she thought, and was astonished by the feeling of despair that even considering such an option could produce. It led to other thoughts—like, why? And, is attraction usually this swift-acting or is the man simply stirring up a few hormonal responses to enliven an otherwise boring month? The possibility made Harriet more wary, doubly determined not to give in to whatever it was that was affecting her.

She showered and dressed then crept down the stairs, deciding it was safer to keep right out of his way. Judging from the way her heart was behaving, and from the heat in her body whenever she thought of him, a nunnery might not be a bad idea.

'You're up early,' James remarked as she walked into

the kitchen, and she rose four inches off the floor and screamed.

'What are you doing in here? Trying to scare the life out of me? Why aren't you in bed? Resting? Recuperating?'

She clutched at her chest in an effort to still the frantic beating of her heart, and scowled at him.

'I'm having a cup of coffee,' he said mildly, 'and I've spent too much time in bed lately. What's more,' he continued, his eyes gleaming with merriment in the early morning sunlight, 'it was lonely in my bed.'

'Tough!' Harriet replied, regaining her composure in a hurry when the talk took on suggestive undertones. She was definitely not going to react to his provocation, not going to be a diversion for him to make his time at Gold Creek pass more swiftly. 'I'm up early because I'm going to town. Is there anything you want or need?'

'Not in town,' he murmured.

Damn! I walked straight into that one, she realised, and turned away from the teasing smile and sultry chuckle.

With a pretence of indifference, she opened cupboard doors and examined the contents, making a mental list of what she needed. Then she peered into the foggy depths of the big chest freezer and counted loaves of bread and packets of the bread rolls she sometimes used for lunch.

'There are croissants in here, if you'd like some for your breakfast,' she offered, remembering the 'breakfast' part of their deal. Not that there was a proper deal as yet. It was difficult to broach the subject of money. 'And there's the strawberry jam Mrs Jenkins brought in on Thursday. It'd be delicious on them.'

'How often to you go to town?'

Being asked a question when there should have been an answer brought her head up out of the freezer.

'As rarely as possible,' she admitted ruefully. 'I

bought this big freezer the week mains power was connected to the town so I stock up about once a month, although sometimes, if I'm lucky, I can go two months. The service station opposite the pub keeps a little bit of everything but it's an expensive way to shop on a regular basis.'

'So are you forced to make this trip because you've got an uninvited guest, eating his way through your supplies?' James asked.

'No way! This visit was already overdue when you arrived,' she assured him, not adding that she suspected she'd have found an excuse to run away to town even if it hadn't been. 'And, as well as shopping, I've an order from the medical supplies people in Sydney, waiting for me at the chemist there. I like to collect it myself so I can check what they've forgotten to send and make it up out of Ron's supplies.'

James grinned with delight at her words. 'You don't have much faith in your medical suppliers?'

'I don't have much faith in any of them,' Harriet told him, closing the freezer door and hoping she'd remember what she needed. 'I once ordered sutures and got a box containing two dozen pairs of scissors in their place, ordered gauze dressings and received slings. So now I don't leave town until every item is checked off against my order form. What's more, if anything's missing I phone them up from Ron's phone and that saves the practice money.'

His grin gave way to an appreciative hoot of laughter and Harriet found herself smiling. There was something seductive in being able to make a man laugh.

'Did you decide if you wanted croissants?' she asked, switching from seduction to food when she realised how far her thoughts had strayed.

'No, I'll stick to toast,' he said, but the half-smile that accompanied the words made Harriet wonder if toast had connotations she hadn't yet discovered.

The thought made her blush and she hurriedly grabbed a pen and a piece of paper and transferred the list to it, mumbled something about hoping he could amuse himself and said goodbye.

'Not eating breakfast before you go?' he asked, the words more provocative than concerned.

'I'll grab a cup of coffee when I get to town,' she said, and kept walking, not too fast but definitely not too slowly, away from this man who was disrupting her life.

It wasn't until she was driving over the top of the hill on the way out of town that she realised she hadn't switched the phone across to her cellphone. Anyone ringing the medical emergency number would get her house—get James. Would he tell the caller to try her cellphone? The number was there on a list on the kitchen wall.

Or would he take the call himself? Go jolting over these rough dirt roads in that stupid red speed machine he called a car? And that reminded her that she'd never asked him the details of his accident. Had speed been a factor? And who had been driving?

It doesn't matter, she told herself. It's none of your business and you don't want to start caring about this man. He'll be gone in a month and will never travel over a dirt road again so he certainly won't be darkening your doorstep! In fact, he could be gone, at least for weekends, in less than a month. If he looked after himself and didn't take on jobs he didn't need to tackle.

Perhaps she should phone him and ask him to switch the calls across—it was as simple as pushing a button on her answering machine.

Her thoughts had reached this stage when she saw the cars stopped on the road ahead. She knew immediately it meant trouble as this was a particularly narrow section of the road where the drop to the river below was at its steepest.

'Harry, thank God it's you!' one of the gathering

called to her as she pulled up and slid out of her car. 'Car's gone over and this young kid climbed up to get help, but the poor little bugger's passed out on us and we don't know what to do with him. Someone's been on the blower and there's an ambulance and tow truck on the way.'

She made her way swiftly towards where a woman knelt beside the prone figure of a child.

'I know enough first aid to know he's breathing,' she said, as Harriet knelt beside her.

'And to keep him warm,' Harriet said, smiling at the woman whose voice was shaky with shock.

But she'd been right about the breathing. The little boy, who looked about eight, was breathing with no raspy sounds indicative of lung or chest damage. His pulse was fast but not abnormally so, Harriet decided, and there was no blood that she could see. She began a physical examination, using touch and sight, her fingers finding a soft swelling on his head which could have led to slight concussion.

Delayed concussion? She thought of stories of people being knocked out, then getting up and walking around for a while before passing out again. Behaviour typifying haematoma—epidural haematoma. Her mind raced through the possibilities, but when she felt the deformity in the child's shoulder and heard the slight crackling sound of crepitus as bone touched bone she guessed that pain from a broken clavicle had caused the little boy to pass out.

'How he climbed back up to the road, I can't imagine,' she muttered, finding scissors in her bag and cutting away the child's T-shirt from his neck so she could check for any indication that blood vessels had been damaged. There was no sign of bruising as yet so she reached for his wrist, wanting to double check with a radial pulse.

'Harry! Over here!'.

Satisfied that the child was in no immediate danger, she left him with the caring woman and headed to where a group of men gathered at the edge of the precipitous drop.

'Art Himstead climbed down.' Graham Nash, a teacher at the local school, had appointed himself organiser of the rescue. He was holding a cellphone to his ear and relaying information to Harriet from Art. 'There's a man and a woman in the car—a big four-wheel-drive Landcruiser. The chap's unconscious but he's breathing, Art says. It's the woman who's worse off.'

Harriet peered tentatively over the cliff, unable to believe anyone could have dropped that far and not been killed. She saw immediately what had happened. The car had come to rest against a boulder that protruded from the rockface, like the huge claw of some prehistoric beast, but Harriet knew how unstable these cliffs could be and she wondered if the claw would hold the car for long enough for them to rescue the two injured occupants.

'If we move the car will it cause more injuries to either of the occupants?' Harriet asked, wondering if they could winch the vehicle up to solid ground before they began treatment.

Graham relayed the question and Harriet felt the air grow still as those gathered waited for a reply.

'There's something piercing the woman's thigh.' Graham repeated Art's words. 'Someone will have to free her before she or the car can be lifted up.'

Harriet felt her stomach clench but she seized the phone from Graham and spoke sharply to Art.

'Don't try to move the woman,' she ordered. 'If there's a lot of blood coming from the wound try to stop it with a pressure pad—roll up your shirt and hold it tightly against it.'

'There's not much blood, Harry, just this dirty great

aerial root through the door of the car and right through her leg.'

'Is she conscious?' Harriet asked.

'Moaning but not talking to me,' Art replied, and Harriet felt a wave of gratitude that someone as relaxed and knowledgeable as Art had been one of the first on the scene.

'We'll have to cut through the root on both sides of her leg to get her free, then leave it in place until we can get her to hospital,' she told Art. 'The ambulance is on the way and the tow truck's just arrived. It'll have cutting gear, and once he's had a look Bob will know how best to deal with both the vehicle and the patients.'

Harriet passed the phone back to Graham with relief. Bob Walters, who ran the local tow truck, was a mountain climber in his spare time. Accidents like this were in his sphere of expertise. Her relief was short-lived. Bob took one look at the precariously perched vehicle, listened to Graham's explanation of what they knew so far and turned to Harriet.

'I daren't try to winch it up from there with injured people inside. One hitch and they'd both go plummeting to the bottom. You'll have to come down with me and give the woman pain relief, then I'll cut the root away from her and we'll bring her up as soon as the ambulance arrives.'

He must have seen her shudder for he patted her affectionately on the shoulder and said, 'Come on, Harry, it's not as bad as the time we had to lower you down that old mine shaft. Now get your gear while I rope up and then I'll fix a sling for you and we'll go together. We'll keep clear of the car for the descent and swing across when we get down.'

Great! Harriet muttered to herself as she prepared a morphine injection for her patient. So it's not as bad as a mine shaft! At least the mine shaft was dark and I couldn't see what was happening, whereas this...

She ventured a look over the cliff and was shuddering again when the throaty roar of an engine made her look up. The shiny red sports car growled to a halt and she watched James Hepworth clamber out awkwardly.

'The call came through to the house. How bad is it?' he demanded as he walked towards her.

'There's a young kid up here with what I suspect is a fractured clavicle, and his parents are in the car. I'm just going down to give the woman morphine before the men cut her free.'

'You can't go down there,' he argued. 'It's ridiculous to expect a woman to dangle over that cliff.'

'It's my job,' Harriet reminded him. 'What I'm trained for. She has a tree root through her thigh—I thought we should leave it in place.'

'Definitely leave it in place,' he said, peering over the edge of the road and frowning darkly. 'But I'll go down there, not you.'

'Oh, act your age,' Harriet snapped. 'This isn't the time for chivalry. You get down there and bang your hip and we'll have to haul up three patients instead of two.'

James glowered at her so fiercely she felt her skin burn in response, but she tilted her chin and said, 'I've prepared morphine and I've got another ampoule in case it's needed, also ligatures, bandages, pads and dressings and a scalpel to cut through the seat belt. What else?'

As she spoke she patted the belt she'd fitted around her waist. It was made of thick webbing and had numerous pockets and loops for carrying supplies and equipment. She'd purchased it after a previous accident where they'd had to climb up—not down—a cliff and had needed to carry the minimum requirements because of weight.

'If you need anything else we can send it down,' James reminded her gruffly, not actually conceding her point but accepting that it was she who should go.

Yet he continued to hover over her as she slipped into

the sling Bob had fashioned for her, and stood beside
the truck as the winch slowly unwound, allowing her to
begin her abseil down the slabbed wall of rock that
dropped into the chasm.

'Go and look at the child,' she reminded him as she
backed cautiously over the edge. He moved—but reluctantly, she felt—to do her bidding.

Then she forgot James as she dropped swiftly, setting
her feet against the wall and pushing outwards to keep
her body clear of the jagged rocks and the scrawny trees
and bushes growing out of them.

'OK, now edge your way to the right,' Art called, and
she realised she must be level with the car. Beside her,
Bob was also dangling over space, but he put his hand
on her arm for reassurance and held her until her feet
found purchase in the rocks and her hands found a bush
that would take her weight.

'We'll stay roped up,' Bob told her, 'but try to find
some solid ground under your feet before you begin to
examine your patients.'

'By solid ground I presume you mean a toe-hold of
some kind,' Harriet complained as she edged towards
the wreck. She'd expected to be scared but adrenalin was
pumping through her body and the concentration she
needed to make her way across the cliff-face left no
room for doubts or fear.

Then Art's hand was reaching out for hers and he
swung her onto the ledge where the claw flattened
slightly like the half-open palm of a hand.

'You're OK now,' Art assured her. 'I reckon if this
ledge was going to go it would have gone by now.'

Harriet noticed the rope he'd tied casually around his
waist before he'd come down and wondered how the
man could be so laid-back about their situation.

'Let's have a look,' she said, wanting nothing more
than to do her job and be hauled back up again.

She pushed past Art and barely smothered her cry of

horror when she saw the woman, pinned in the seat of the car. But was that the only injury?

Looking back up towards the road, she realised that the car hadn't dropped as far as she'd at first supposed and, from the look of it, it hadn't rolled over so crush injuries were unlikely. The vehicle must have had its headlong rush over the edge slowed by the tree whose root had pierced the woman's thigh, then as it broke off that restraint and toppled again it had hit the jagged protrusion of rock and come to rest almost upright, wedged tightly against the cliff.

Harriet clambered up onto the bonnet and reached in through the broken windscreen. The woman was breathing shallowly and her pulse racing—shock was setting in. Treat for shock and then pain?

'The doc says get her up, then treat for shock,' Art told her. 'If the car goes you won't save her anyway so remove her from the danger. Same with the man. He says the ambulance should be here soon with equipment to stabilise their spines and necks, and as soon as you've done that get them out of here.'

Harriet nodded, beyond surprise that James could be answering her unspoken questions over Art's cellphone.

The woman was moaning again, but blood on her head made Harriet hesitate. She couldn't get close enough to determine if it was from a flesh wound but she knew for certain that opiates like morphine should be used with caution on head-injured patients. Before she could decide, a shout from above suggested that the ambulance had arrived.

'Let's get the man out first,' Bob suggested. 'I don't want to put extra weight in the vehicle with both of them in it, but once he's gone I can get up on the bonnet and cut the root away inside the door. Are you going to knock her out?'

It wasn't the best choice of words but Harriet knew what he meant. Leaning in as far as she could, she lifted first one of the women's eyelids and then the other, and decided one pupil was slightly dilated.

'No!' she said firmly. 'Let's get them both up to the top and let the doctor decide how to treat them.'

She turned as an ambulance attendant came dangling down to join them, and was pleased when Bob took the phone and ordered those directing things above to pull Art up.

'We'll have the whole damn town down here at this rate,' he complained, but Harriet was glad to have the attendant's professional help as they fitted a cervical collar around the driver's neck and eased him into a short spinal board to immobilise his spine, before lifting him out of the seat.

'Strange way to have ended up,' the ambulance attendant pointed out as he checked that the man's legs and feet weren't tangled or obstructed. 'I'd have thought the engine would have come back in on top of him when they hit this rock.'

'I think they've come at it sideways,' Harriet told him. 'Definitely the best way for the car to fall because of the new inbuilt safety zones to minimise damage from side-on collisions.'

They strapped the man into a safety harness and eased him out of the seat.

'We'll never get him on to a stretcher down here—there's just no room. I'll take him up.'

The attendant relayed this decision through his two-way, then positioned the unconscious man so he could protect his body from further injury on the way up.

'Take us up,' he called through the mouthpiece that jutted out in front of his lips, 'but do it bloody slowly. I'm not too good at this game.'

Harriet found herself smiling. She knew exactly how the man felt but knew that, in an emergency, you did what you had to do.

'I'd like to get the woman secured to a sling before

we cut anything,' she told Bob, and again they waited while more equipment was lowered. Then Harriet crawled into the driver's seat and fitted the collar, followed by a short spine board, slipping it in behind the woman before strapping it firmly into place.

'I'm going to clip a safety harness around you,' she told her patient, 'then we'll cut you free.'

She hoped she sounded more confident than she felt, although she doubted the woman heard or cared. If the rock gave way she'd have trouble getting herself out and she hated to think what might happen to her patient.

'OK, I've got the vehicle secured,' Bob called to her. 'She's hooked up to the big winch on the truck so if the rock goes hang onto the seat and someone will haul us all up.'

'Thanks for that very comforting remark,' Harriet muttered, bending low to make sure the woman's feet were free when they did begin to move her. 'How about we get this root cut off and get out of here before that happens?'

Bob climbed up on the bonnet and produced a small hacksaw. Leaning in over the dashboard, he proceeded to cut through the two-inch diameter root. Harriet held it where it disappeared into the woman's leg, trying to steady it as much as possible in order to minimise internal damage. The woman cried out, then sighed and relaxed as unconsciousness claimed her.

The ambulance attendant returned as they completed the job, bringing tools to force the passenger door open so they could take the woman out from that side.

'You'll have to cut the root on the other side of her leg as well,' Harriet told Bob. 'It disappears into the centre console and I've no idea how long it is.'

Bob leaned in again and the sawing began. While he worked, the door was opened and the ambulance attendant unclipped the safety line Harriet had put on the woman and clipped on one attached to his harness so once again he and his patient could be lifted in tandem.

'OK, she's free,' Harriet told him, and helped him shift the woman's weight out of the car.

Fifteen minutes later Harriet was back on the road, her knees shaking so much from reaction she'd have collapsed if James hadn't caught and held her.

'You need to sit down,' he said roughly, half leading, half carrying her towards his car.

'I'm all right,' she protested. 'Look after the woman. She was very shocked—I should have started fluids for her before we got her out. I didn't give her morphine because her head was bleeding but you'll be able to tell—'

'Harriet!'

He said her name with such firm insistence that she stopped babbling and looked at him. His brown eyes were studying her face intently and he was frowning so she smiled to see if that might make his frown go away. It didn't. In fact, if anything, it intensified it.

'The ambulance has gone,' he told her, pressing her down so her knees gave way and she collapsed into the low-slung seat of his ridiculous vehicle. 'I put her on a drip as soon as she came up to the top. I think you're right about possible head injury, the man seemed OK but, again, he could have struck his head as the car rolled. We've done all we can—or at least you've done most of it while I've waited at the top like a useless lump of protoplasm.'

Even in her confused state Harriet heard the bitterness in his voice.

'You shouldn't even be here,' she pointed out. 'If I'd switched the phone through, like I usually do, you wouldn't have known about the accident.'

She was looking up at him, her eyes a very dark blue in the paleness of her face. James felt a slight lurch in his intestines and reached out to touch the bright hair.

'I thought it might have been you when the caller said a car had gone over just out of town. The timing was about right!'

He watched surprise shadow her eyes and wished he'd kept his mouth shut, but the memory of the nerve-racking drive from Harriet's house to here would remain with him for a long time.

'You were worried it was me?' she repeated, frowning as she tried to assimilate the words.

He could sense her uneasiness, as if his concern was regenerating itself inside her. Trying to make less of it, he shrugged.

'Well, imagine me trying to get the home visits done in this little job if you'd banged up your trusty old Jeep!'

'So it was only the car you were worried about?' Harriet asked, and he was pleased to see colour seeping back into her cheeks and a sparkle returning to her eyes.

'Of course,' he lied smoothly, unwilling to think about his own reactions now that all had ended well enough. 'Do you want me to drive you home and get someone else to bring your car?'

'Drive me home?' Harriet retorted, straightening in the seat and fixing him with one of her more militant glares. 'I'm on my way to town.'

Once again James felt an unfamiliar uneasiness and wondered why he should feel protective towards her. If he'd learnt one thing in the few days he'd been in Gold Creek it was that Sister Bossy Logan was more than capable of looking after herself.

Yet he heard himself, against all common sense, saying, 'Harriet, you've been through a draining mental and physical ordeal. You should rest, but if you insist on going to town let me drive you. I'll take your car—I'll admit it probably handles the roads around here better than mine—'

He stopped abruptly as the cause of his concern leaned forward in the car and covered her face with her hands.

He could see her shoulders shaking and he crouched down, cursing the pain that stabbed through his thigh and reaching out to take her in his arms.

'What's wrong? Are you hurt? Why are you crying?'

But as he touched her shoulders she looked up and he saw the merriment in her eyes and tears of laughter, not pain, streaking through the dust on her cheeks.

'Oh, James,' she said unsteadily. 'It's nice to think you're concerned about me but I promise you I don't fall apart that easily. And I'm only laughing because I had a bet with myself that you'd never admit—to me at least—that it was a mistake to bring this red terror to Gold Creek.'

'And to think I felt sorry for you,' he fumed, as angry with himself for showing his concern as with her for refusing to accept it. 'This red terror, as you call it, is currently providing you with a seat. I should have left you in a heap on the ground and let the ants bite you.'

Weak effort, he told himself, but it had seemed important to have the last word, especially as his hip was about to give way and he would probably collapse back onto the road any moment.

She must have sensed his pain again for her laughter subsided and she put out her hand and touched his forearm.

'I'm sorry you were worried, and even sorrier you had to drive down here because I was careless and forgot to switch the phone over,' she said gently, but then she smiled and her eyes gleamed again as she added, 'But get up now or your pelvis will collapse and all your new bone growth will break apart. I don't need an extra patient on my books.'

Harriet watched him ease himself stiffly upright and kept her smile in place, although she could almost feel his pain. She'd been pleased by his concern earlier, but had told herself the reaction was ridiculous for someone who claimed she treasured her independence. Her confusion had made her laugh and when he'd knelt beside her her body had rebelled, wanting only to lean towards his as willow branches leant towards a stream.

So she'd teased him and now that he was gone she could admit that he'd been right—reaction was setting in and her legs were weak, her fingers trembling and it would be madness to risk the road to town in this condition.

As she watched him walk away to speak to the men who were still directing traffic around the accident site she contemplated admitting he'd been right, and groaned quietly to herself. Then she considered spending the entire day in his company—and probably all of Sunday as well—and groaned again.

Bob, who'd been walking past, turned towards her.

'I'm towing the wreck into town if you want to hitch a lift. I can give you an hour or so to do your shopping while I fix up the paperwork and contact the insurers, then I'll run you back. Art was walking in to collect his car when he saw the boy. Left it at the pub last night. He'll take your heap of junk home for you.'

Harriet hesitated, but only for an instant. Even a short reprieve, a few hours when she could legitimately avoid her house guest, were better than none at all.

'Thanks, Bob,' she said, standing up and heading towards the tow truck. 'Could you let the doctor know I'm going?'

Which was a cowardly, but necessary, way to escape!

CHAPTER SEVEN

IT WAS mid-afternoon before Harriet returned home to a silent house. The red car was parked outside her front door behind her own old wreck, but of the doctor there was no sign.

Pleased and disappointed in about equal measure, Harriet lugged her bags of groceries into the kitchen, then dragged the medical equipment just inside the front door. She'd take it down to the surgery later.

She unpacked, restocking her cupboards and trying to ignore the unusual purchases like stuffed olives, devilled nuts and fancy chocolate biscuits which thoughts of James had prompted her to buy.

As she rolled up the last plastic bag she noticed a piece of paper flutter to the floor. Bending down to retrieve it, she recognised the upright slashes of James's writing.

Friends arrived and have whisked me off to visit the vineyards. They have a station wagon and I'll be ensconced on the back seat with leg stretched out, suitably padded and pampered. Don't expect me back tonight.

James

After reading the words three times and realising they weren't going to change, Harriet sighed, crumpled the note into a tight ball and shied it at the bin. It missed so she kicked it around the kitchen floor for a while, sighed again and walked upstairs.

At least he'd only be jolting over rough roads for half

an hour on the back way to the vineyards. Wine attracted even more tourists than gold so the vineyard area had slightly better roads. Not that she cared where he went or how much it hurt his injuries! With the weekend restored to her, she could paint the second bedroom at the front of the house and get it ready for the spring influx of tourists.

The thought thrilled her about as much as the idea of colonic irrigation, a practice she'd been reading of in a natural health magazine.

He returned next evening, dropped off by an exceptionally good-looking couple in smart 'country weekend' clothes. Harriet watched them from the upstairs bedroom where she'd just finished pasting a flowered border around the walls.

The woman kissed him, but as a friend, Harriet decided. James disappeared from view as he stepped up onto her verandah and the couple returned to their car, waved and called goodbyes then drove away.

Harriet waited, wanting him to acknowledge her existence—her ownership of the house—but all she heard was a shuffling noise followed by a heavy thud, which made her leave her sanctuary and go rushing down the steps.

'Don't tell me,' James groaned as he heard her clattering approach. 'I should have stayed at home and rested. I should have told Julie and Mike I was in more pain than they realised.'

He looked up at her from where he'd landed just inside the door and his eyes pleaded not for sympathy but understanding. But his pain had upset her too much to listen to any pleas and as she knelt beside him she let her rage boil over.

'You stupid, stupid man! You're supposed to be a doctor! And what happened to the padding and pampering? What have you done? Have you dislocated something, broken the new bone apart? Oh, how could you be so idiotic?'

She was feeling at his thigh, near to tears with exasperation and concern, so when he touched her lightly on her cheek she pulled away and stared at him, brought up short—bewildered—by the sensations his fingers fired so easily.

'I've not damaged the bones,' he said quietly, 'but I think I overworked muscles that have been idle too long. It's a muscle spasm, that's all. I'll be OK eventually.'

'Eventually!' Harriet snorted, so relieved she wanted to hug him but knew she shouldn't—couldn't! 'And how long is eventually?'

He smiled at her and predictably her heart went into its mad cavorting act, but common sense told her he couldn't stay here in the doorway while he waited for the pain to go away, while self-knowledge added that doing something practical was the best way to hide her body's behaviour.

'Can you make it as far as your room?' she asked. 'A muscle spasm should respond to massage so if you lie on your bed...'

She found it impossible to say any more, thoughts of beds and James in juxtaposition producing more interior disturbance. Instead, she helped him to his feet and supported him as he limped towards his bedroom.

'I'll get some oil,' she muttered when he'd finally made it to the bed and had collapsed on it, groaning and moving restlessly as he tried to ease the pain.

'You don't have to do this!' he growled at her when she returned with towels and a bottle of scented bath oil.

'No, I don't,' she agreed. 'I could go into the kitchen and enjoy my evening meal, without giving a thought to your pain, but I think I promised something when they gave me my degree. We nurses don't do your Hippocratic oath thing but we do have certain responsibilities to our fellow humans.'

She was talking to hide her own misgivings about what she was about to do and her mind kept demanding why the man couldn't have injured his forearm and not his thigh.

Not that she'd ever considered thighs as particularly intimate parts of the body, but they sure came close to some disturbing bits—

She switched her mind away from such thoughts and surveyed her patient.

'Undo your belt and zipper and I'll yank your trousers off for you.' She hoped the words sounded brusque enough to kill any suggestive undertones.

'Now there's an offer few men could resist,' James retorted, but when Harriet sneaked a look at his face it was drained and tired-looking, his eyes closed and his mouth shut tightly against the pain.

She removed his shoes and while he lifted his hips off the bed she eased his trousers off and gasped when she saw the network of scars on his upper leg and hip.

'Banishes all sexy thoughts, doesn't it?' he muttered drily, and she heard the self-mockery in his voice.

'Makes me realise just how extensive your injuries were,' she told him, reaching for the towels she'd wet and then warmed in the microwave. She hoped she sounded blasé about it, but in her heart she was wondering just how emotionally affected by the scarring a handsome, virile man like James would be.

'These are hot,' she warned as she covered his upper thigh with the folded towels. Her thoughts meandered on, leading to women and why there'd been no phone calls to or from some lover or love interest. 'Heat should relax the muscle before I begin to massage.'

He nodded, seemingly beyond caring what she did to his body. She removed the towels and poured oil into her hand, the scars distracting her attention from the black underpants stretched across his pelvic region.

His skin was tight, the muscles bunched beneath it,

and she realised he was as tense as she was, as wary about this treatment as she was of giving it.

'Relax,' she told him. 'Think of water washing across the beach or wind rustling in the trees or whatever other thoughts might help your body release its tension.'

She ran her hands from his knee to his upper thigh then brought them down again, moving lightly over the scarred tissue but pressing more firmly into the muscle. It became a rhythmic repetition and each time she kneaded a little more deeply, pressing harder on the knots she found, easing off then returning to them— trying to keep her mind on the patient, not the man.

But they can't be separated, the distracting voice in her head suggested, and she knew she needed more than will-power to keep her thoughts from straying. She studied the track of the scars in his leg, and examined the ones above the strip of black material.

'Just how badly did you injure your hip and femur?' she asked, pleased to have found a distraction.

'Badly!' he said gruffly. 'In fact, if you promise to keep working that magic on my muscles I'll tell you about it.'

Harriet was surprised by this promise of co-operation and she wondered if James, too, needed distraction. As heat flared in her body she concentrated more fiercely on the still-taut muscles, refusing to raise her eyes beyond a certain imaginary line she'd drawn near the top of his leg.

'As you so cleverly diagnosed, I was in a side-on accident. The other vehicle was a truck running a red light. The driver of the car I was in took off as the light turned green, without noticing this idiot coming at us. He slammed into the passenger door and the impact squeezed me between the door and the raised area between the bucket seats. Unfortunately, something had to give.'

His body reacted to the memory with a convulsive

shiver and Harriet's fingers became gentler for a moment, soothing instead of massaging, until he breathed deeply and began to talk again.

'What gave was one wing of the ilium, quite close to the sacroiliac joint, and the head of my femur, which pushed everything out of place before it finally snapped.'

'Greater trochanter,' Harriet said softly, remembering the knobbly head of the femur from the list of bones she'd recited over and over again when studying the yellowed old skeleton at university. 'Did they pin it?'

'Pinned everything they could find, I think. There was a second fracture in the femur, in the lower third, which served to complicate things. The idea of pinning is to get patients weight-bearing as soon as possible, but I'm no lightweight to bear and the pelvic fracture remained unstable so it was traction and lying immobile, then the dreaded hip spica cast, then—'

'An unbearably long convalescence,' Harriet finished for him.

'Don't start feeling sorry for me at this stage,' he told her gruffly. 'I deal much better with brisk, no-nonsense orders and a total lack of sympathy.'

'I bet!' Harriet muttered. 'If you'd followed orders you wouldn't be lying here in pain right now.'

He shifted slightly and she glanced up to see him smiling.

'But then I'd have missed out on this most wonderful experience, Sister Logan.' He paused, and added, 'Wouldn't I?'

The words crept into her head, and she straightened abruptly.

'I'll reheat the towels and bring them back. You should leave them on for a while to keep the muscle warm and relaxed, then sit up and work it slowly so it doesn't cramp up again.'

She grasped the towels and was heading out the door when he said, 'Scared you'll need to do it again?'

Pretending she hadn't heard, she kept moving, but scared didn't begin to describe how she felt. As his skin and muscle had moved beneath her fingers her mind had drifted into deep and dangerous fantasies—notions of her fingers drifting higher to where dark hair curled up from his inner thighs, forming a nest—

'Stop it!' she scolded herself as she folded the towels and put them in the microwave. 'That man is not for you! Imagine how Doug would feel if he returned to work to find you'd had a brief fling with his old friend when you've said no to him a hundred and eighty times. Or was it a hundred and eighty-two?'

She stared out of the window, lost in thought. Yes, Doug would be upset, but not as upset as she would be—with herself mainly—for giving in to a little lustful urging, for that was all it could possibly be! But how long had it been since she'd felt a lustful urge? the inner temptress whispered. And how long before another might present itself? With a ragged sigh she retrieved the towels and headed back to temptation's bedroom.

'I usually just have toast and something on Sunday nights,' she announced, to show she hadn't been at all affected by the intimacy of the massage. 'That do you?'

He was hitched up against the pillows and he reached out and took the towels out of her hands and spread them on his thigh again.

'Give me ten minutes with the towels, another ten for a hot shower and I'll take you up to the pub for dinner.'

Harriet stared at him, her mind scrabbling desperately for an excuse but failing to find one.

'Don't stand there, thinking up an argument,' he chided. 'Get upstairs and put on something pretty and we'll paint the old town red!'

She grinned at the thought and said, 'All ten houses of it?' But she turned away, still smiling, and found herself hurrying up the stairs, wondering what she owned that he'd class as pretty.

By the time she reached the top of the steps common sense had returned and she settled on a pair of jeans and a soft, dark blue, mohair jumper that had been a favourite garment for so long it was like a second skin.

The word 'pretty' lingered long enough for her to draw a fine line of midnight-blue eye-liner along her upper lid and dash a bit of mascara on her lashes. Instead of gloss, she put on lipstick, a subtle golden red that didn't clash too wildly with her hair.

Her hair! She dragged a brush ruthlessly through the curls, willing them to sit down, but all it did was make them bounce more wilfully around her head so they formed a shining nimbus and made her skin look pale and her eyes a darker blue.

'Not pretty but not unattractive,' she decided, slipping on a pair of flat-heeled shoes and heading for the steps. But at the top she remembered another of Elly's presents and she hurried back into her bedroom and searched along the top shelf of her cupboard until she found it.

Be! The modern, aggressive Calvin Klein perfume she rarely used because Doug had allergies. She sprayed a little on her wrist then puffed it in the air and turned in the droplets, letting them catch her here and there so the fragrance would follow her as she moved.

The phone rang as she reached the bottom of the steps and, as she'd guessed, her dinner at the pub was off.

'It's Maud again,' she told James when he emerged from his room and looked enquiringly at her. 'You go on up to the hotel and get your dinner. I'll join you later if I can.' She gave him a regretful smile. 'Maybe in time for the town-painting!'

But as she headed for the door, grabbing her case and the cellphone off the hall table as she passed, he picked up his bag and followed her.

'I'll come with you,' he said. 'She hasn't been back to see me and I'm wondering if it's because she knew she was getting worse.'

'You don't have to come,' she told him, angered by her own disappointment that their plans had been disrupted. 'Doug's never here on Sundays so I'd normally have handled this on my own anyway, and I'd already decided that next time it happened I'd phone for an ambulance. Once she's in hospital she'll be forced to have the tests.'

'You can't force a patient to do anything, even in hospital,' he reminded her, following her to the car and climbing in before she could object again. 'And maybe her reasons to not have them are valid.'

'You didn't think so last week,' Harriet argued.

'Last week I was a different person.'

Harriet turned to stare at him, swung her attention back to her driving in time to avoid a family, walking down the middle of the road, then said, 'What on earth do you mean by that remark? Different in what way?'

James knew he'd diverted her and he smiled as he admitted, 'Different in that I was looking at people as the illness or condition first. I don't know just when I started to do it and didn't realise it had become a habit until you accused me of it one day when you were angry. I thought about it later and discovered it was true. The stay in hospital should have humanised the whole business of medicine for me but all it did was aggravate me, but meeting the people who come into the surgery— seeing kids like Kate, having to grow up before her time—I'm different.'

He saw her glance his way again then turn back to the road, and he thought how attractive her profile was with its long, straight forehead, its slightly uptilted nose and firm—possibly stubborn—chin.

'And, being different, you'd let Maud forego the tests?' she demanded. 'Damn it, James, she's only sixty!'

She swung the car into the drive that led to the tiny house and turned off the engine. 'Unless she's sitting up, talking, I'm going to phone for an ambulance,' she told him, belligerence in every line of her body.

He chuckled at her vehemence, the evidence of her commitment to these patients who were also friends.

'I agree,' he told her. 'And I've already suggested to her that she has the tests and then, when the doctors know what's wrong, decide if she wants the treatment.'

Harriet felt her racing pulses slow. He stirred her up deliberately, making out he didn't care when he was usually two thoughts ahead of her. It was part of what she liked about him, this thinking past the present to the next stage in a patient's treatment. She waved to Bert and headed for the house.

Although liking James and having lustful thoughts about him were fairly widely removed, she reminded herself.

'She's been like this for ten minutes,' Bert greeted them. 'I got Pat next door to phone you and came straight back.'

'Phone for the ambulance, Harriet,' James ordered as he knelt beside Maud, who appeared to be unconscious but was shaking uncontrollably. 'I'm going to put in a catheter and start normal saline and give her diazepam in that to begin with. It should stop the seizure activity and keep her stable for about twenty minutes. Had Doug checked her for hypoglycaemia?'

'He tested her for diabetes when she had the first attack,' Harriet told him when she'd made the call. Kneeling beside Maud, she taped the catheter into place so sudden movement wouldn't dislodge it. 'But we always saw her after the seizures, never like this.'

Satisfied with the taping, she turned back to James, 'Twenty minutes won't get her to town. Should I go with her to continue treatment?'

She watched James start the flow of saline, and held her breath as he began to inject the drug into the liquid.

She knew how insoluble the diazepam was in water and how important it was to infuse it slowly.

'No, Bert should go with her,' he said, his voice barely audible. 'We'll know if she's going to suffer any respiratory distress as a result of the drug before she leaves here, and if necessary I'll put her on oxygen.' He looked up at Harriet.

'Could you go down to the surgery and bring back a small canister and a soft nasal cannula, just in case? And I think I noticed Doug had some phenytoin in solution there. Bring back...' he paused and Harriet could see him doing rapid sums in his head '...a pack of five ampoules. It's all packed with 50mg per millilitre and I think I saw a pack of five 5ml ampoules, each containing 250mg. I can infuse that slowly through the saline and it will take over from the diazepam.'

Harriet hesitated but when James looked up again she understood the gravity of Maud's condition and left without an argument.

'I brought back more saline as well,' Harriet told James when she got back, setting down the things he'd asked for and the squashy bag of fluid.

James nodded, but the tension in his face told her he was still worried, a worry that hadn't eased by the time the ambulance arrived. Maud had stopped shaking, but until blood tests were done it would be impossible to tell if the drugs were holding her stable or if the seizure activity had ceased.

Harriet had taken Bert into the bedroom and was supervising him while he put together clothes for himself and Maud. James eased himself up on to a chair and looked down at the woman who had been his first 'real' patient for a long time.

'I'd like to go with you,' he told her quietly as he heard the ambulance pull up outside, 'but I've a feeling Sister Logan will read me the riot act and tell me my first duty is to the other patients here, although she'd go like a shot herself if I don't convince her with the same argument.'

The ambulance attendants came in, the noisy metal gurney rattling between them.

'Can one of you two keep a timed infusion going in this drip line?' James asked, and saw both men bridle as if he'd hurt their pride.

'I'm sorry,' he muttered. 'I'm feeling bad because I'd like to go with Maud myself.'

'Just like Harry!' the older man remarked. 'Can't believe that anyone else can look after her patients even a quarter as well as she can! What are you giving her?'

'Phenytoin-dilantin,' James explained, considerably heartened by the man's remarks. 'It's tricky stuff, no more than 50mg a minute so each ampoule should take five minutes to go in.'

The young attendant smiled at his colleague. 'Reckon we might just about be able to manage that,' he drawled. 'How much altogether?'

'Guessing at her weight, I'd say the correct dose for Maud would be about 1350mg. We've got five ampoules of 250mg so, hopefully, that will hold her until you get to town.'

James helped the two men lift the recumbent woman onto the gurney. He was surprised at the ease with which they operated and realised from their expertise that they must practise safe lifting techniques as part of their training.

'Have you asked if Bert can go with them?' Harriet asked as she emerged from the bedroom. 'And, Bert, if you don't stop fussing about watering the garden and feeding the hens I'll hit you. I'll arrange it for you and, yes, I'll take the milk out of the fridge before it can go sour and I'll phone the hospital and ask them to arrange accommodation in town for you.'

She bustled the small man in front of her and James

hid a smile. He might tease her by calling her Sister Bossy, but what she did was out of love and affection for her patients, and at times like this he suspected bossiness was a lot more effective than sympathy.

'You're concerned about her, aren't you?' she asked as they watched the ambulance depart.

'Very,' he confirmed. 'That's why I wanted Bert to go. I checked her file after the last visit and noticed that the incidents have been coming closer together. It suggests a fast-growing tumour of some kind.'

James saw her close her eyes and realised how impossible it must be to maintain professional distance from patients in a community of this size. Realised, too, that he was affected by her distress—that he wanted to comfort her. He rested his hand gently on her shoulder.

'She made her decision about this a long time ago—back when she first ignored Doug's advice to go for tests,' he said gently.

Harriet lifted her head and he saw a fragile smile flutter for an instant on her lips.

'Never could tell Maud anything!' she said, then she blinked back her tears and turned resolutely away from him. 'I'm afraid it will be toast and something for dinner after all,' she said in a determinedly bright voice. 'The dining room at the hotel will be shut. Do you want to take the car home? I'll clean up here before I go and see there's water for Bert's precious chickens.'

So much for comforting her! For a moment there he'd thought she might have given way to her sadness but, no, Sister Logan was made of sterner stuff. She'd clean up any mess and water hens and organise his supper, but she wouldn't cry.

'I'll clean up here,' he offered, as the ammonia smell of urine made him realise what she'd meant about the cleaning. 'You do the hens. You'll be more familiar with the geography of the back yard.'

She spun back and stared at him, as if staggered by his suggestion.

'I'm not totally useless,' he told her. 'And I have mopped floors before today.'

This time her smile was wider, more relaxed, and she shook her head in disbelief.

'Now why should I find that hard to accept?' she said. 'The mop and bucket are outside the back door, there's cleaning stuff under the sink and I'll be back to inspect the job as soon as I've checked on Bert's babies.'

Harriet headed for the door, her concern for Maud now overlaid by some subtle shift in the balance between herself and James. Surely not because he'd seen her distress? Or because of her own realisation that he cared not only as a doctor but as a person?

She made her way towards the chicken coop, glad of the moonlight now flooding the land. All was quiet and the tub of water reflected the night sky, but she didn't hurry back towards the house. She needed time to think.

'Come on, I'm done and I've checked the refrigerator. The milk was the only thing that might go off so I've tipped it out.'

Turning towards his voice, she saw him silhouetted in the doorway, a tall dark shadow with a deep sultry voice. A stranger she'd met less than a week ago, a man with polished manners and practised charm, unlike any of the men she knew and most of those she'd met.

'You know, apart from the fact that you had surgical ambitions before your accident, that you can cook—and mop floors—and have a mother who paints, I know nothing about you.'

The words had sounded better in her head than they did hanging in the air between them so she pushed past him and began to shut windows and turn off lights.

'Do you want to know more?' he asked, following her through the tiny house and making it seem even smaller.

'Not particularly,' she replied, and realised she'd spoken the truth. Knowing more about him would be dangerous.

'Then why the sudden listing of what you do know?' he persisted.

'It was your image, dark against the light. We see people but so much of what makes them unique is hidden in the shadows, tucked away in the layers of self that are built up throughout a lifetime.'

They came out into the front garden and Harriet pulled the door shut.

'And getting close to someone means peeling away those layers?' James suggested.

'Probably,' Harriet admitted, sorry she'd ever started this conversation, which was now making her exceedingly tense.

'Shall I tell you more about my life?' he asked temptingly, moving closer so she could see his lips move and the way the moon lit one side of his face, highlighting his profile.

'No!' she said. 'I wasn't asking for that. I don't know why...'

He took another step towards her and she knew it was time to move away, to run—not walk—back to the car and drive immediately to the house where her own surroundings would break the spell the stars and moon had cast about her.

'Sure you don't know why?' he asked, bending towards her and stealing her breath with his lips.

His kisses puzzled her. Even as she accepted the pressure of his mouth on hers and moved to fit her lips more closely, to explore the shape of his and let him know the shape of hers, her mind was trying to analyse what it was that made them different. Not different to Doug's or other kisses she'd sampled—not in a comparative way—but different as kisses went.

Perhaps it was the lack of heat, although heat was there between them. Only a fool would not have recognised that. But it was a different heat, controlled, reined in, as if kissing her was an experiment he needed to carry out under his own terms.

She stepped away from him, breathless but still puzzled for he didn't move to hold her, hadn't touched her with anything but his lips.

'I don't want you doing that!' she muttered at him, bewildered and frustrated by his behaviour.

'OK,' he said, as if her request was easily granted. 'I'll try to desist, but it's not entirely my fault.'

'What do you mean, not entirely your fault? Have I been flinging myself into your arms? Pressing kisses on your lips for no reason whatsoever? Honestly, James Hepworth, you're weird!'

She stormed away from him, heading for the car, and his laughter followed her.

'To tell you the truth, that's exactly how I feel—weird! I don't intend kissing you, you know, it's just that every now and then an irresistible urge overcomes me and I find myself doing it.'

'Well, try harder to resist!' Harriet told him, barely waiting for him to be seated in the vehicle before she took off in a flurry of loose gravel.

CHAPTER EIGHT

MONDAY passed uneventfully with a kind of truce undeclared but still observed between them. Harriet hid behind her most 'efficient nurse' persona and James seemed content to leave her there, no longer trying to entice the other Harriet out to play his teasing games. They ate dinner at the pub and walked the short distance home, Harriet talking non-stop about work as an antidote to the moonlight.

Tuesday morning brought bad news. Maud's tests and scans revealed an inoperable tumour and the gloomy prognosis was making radium treatment unlikely.

As they drove towards Hillview for the afternoon clinic James glanced at his chauffeur. She'd accepted the diagnosis with a tightening of her lips and a suspicious sparkle in her eyes, but she hadn't indulged in useless 'if onlys'. James found his admiration for her increasing.

'It must be one of Australia's most unique villages,' he said as they drove down the long steep hill which gave the town its name. 'In fact, until I saw it I wouldn't have believed such places existed.'

James tried to count the houses, maybe twelve in all, but crammed together, porches sagging over the next-door neighbour's verandah and walls leaning crazily this way and that. And the hectic colours, sky-blue paint on one and crimson on the next, while a tiny store tucked between two larger houses was painted in rainbow stripes, as if the owner had scrounged all the remnants of paint left over from the other decorating efforts.

'A cartoon town to look at,' he added when his companion continued to stare straight ahead, as if driving required all her attention.

Harriet's silence disturbed him but not as much as her lovely mouth, down-turned at the corners, spoiling the profile he found so delightful.

'Maud made her choice,' he reminded her, and her lips tilted upward and she gave a brief nod, confirming that the unspoken regrets had been hammering in her head.

'And knowing that should make it easier,' she admitted as she drew up outside the lilac door that opened into their two-roomed surgery. 'But it doesn't—it hurts. I hurt!'

He was staggered—only acute distress could have made her admit such a thing to him. He half reached out for her then stopped, knowing she'd be even more upset if he gave her a hug in the main street of Hillview.

'Tough Sister Bossy?' he teased instead, and was pleased when her shoulders relaxed and she seemed to shrug off her dark mood.

'That's me,' she agreed, but her rueful smile stabbed him to the heart and his arms ached to hold her.

'Hi, Harry!'

'What's up, Doc?'

The first of their patients began to appear, the casual or joking greetings now more familiar. James took the keys from Harriet and unlocked the door then stood, diverted by the sight of a woman he hadn't seen before, struggling up the street. Something in the way she held her body told him she was in considerable pain and he walked to meet her, introduced himself and held her arm to support her the last few metres.

He asked her name but didn't press for an answer when he realised it was taking all her strength to keep moving. Harriet was waiting outside and she immediately ushered them through the front door, past now-silent patients, motioning to him to take the woman straight through to the consulting room.

'Mary Ogilvie,' Harriet whispered to him, then she pulled the door closed and left him with the stranger.

'OK, who arrived first?' Harriet asked the four patients now standing, talking quietly, in the front room. She hadn't wanted to leave Mary, hurt and embarrassed, waiting with her neighbours, but she was sorry she hadn't had the opportunity to speak to James about Mary's situation.

So she made her list, told the patients it would do them good to wait in the sun on the verandah today and, having herded them out through the door, she moved closer to the thin wall separating the two rooms and listened shamelessly.

'You have to tell me, Mary. We can stop this kind of thing,' she heard James say. 'Don't you realise you could be killed when simple counselling, someone talking to whoever it is, might at least begin to solve the problem?'

Silence told her Mary wasn't going to tell this stranger anything so when James persisted in his questions, speaking of his duty to report the assault to the police, Harriet knew she'd have to act. Picking up the cellphone, she tapped on the door and barged into the room.

'Urgent call for you on this, Doctor,' she said. 'You can take it in the back yard in case it's private. Sorry, Mary!'

She cast an apologetic look towards Mary and all but pushed James through the door that led to the back yard.

'Don't ask her any more questions,' she whispered urgently. 'It's too long a story to tell you now but I'll explain it to you later.'

James frowned at her and she could see his anger in his white-knuckled fists and his darkly furious eyes.

'You dared to interrupt a patient consultation to tell me what to do? That woman's been badly beaten,

Harriet. It's an assault, an offence, and for once we'll do things my way. She needs proper protection, Harriet, not over-protective friends and neighbours trying to hush things up. Today she's only injured, next time she might be dead.'

'I know, we all know,' Harriet told him, desperation sharpening her tone. 'But patch her up and give her pain relief and let her go, James. I'll tell you the whole story as we drive home, and if you still feel you want to report the assault you can phone the police then.'

She looked up into his face, begging him to go along with her advice, but although the anger died away there was little sign of agreement.

'I won't report it immediately,' he relented, but his tone told her that the empathy which had sparked between them earlier was gone. He might joke and call her Sister Bossy but he wasn't a man who took orders easily, especially when they went against his ethical code.

For Harriet the afternoon dragged slowly by, patient numbers few and consultations taking longer than usual so she found herself growing more and more restless. She phoned Phil Gibbes, Mary's neighbour, and was still speaking to her when the last patient departed and James followed him through the door.

'I've locked up in there,' he said abruptly. 'I'll wait for you in the car.'

She watched him stalk out as she listened to Phil recount the previous night's events, noting the deliberately straight back and shoulders, the strict control over his limp. Still angry! Still furious, possibly! Not that she could blame him—it had been a rude, unforgivable thing for her to do.

'OK, Phil, thanks,' she said when the saga had been told and she had all the information she needed. 'You handled it brilliantly, but please remember to call me if you need me.'

Returning the phone to its cradle, she tidied the minute desk, locked the filing cabinet and, unable to find any other delaying tactics, made her way out the door. As she turned to lock it behind her she could feel James's eyes on her back and it took considerable effort not to scurry back inside and put off the confrontation for a little longer.

But he didn't mention her behaviour or her promise, not when she reached the car nor when she started the engine and drove carefully out of town. By the time they were halfway up the hill, Harriet knew he was simply waiting for her explanation and had no intention of saying another word until he'd heard what she had to say.

'Mary's son, Will, suffers from autism,' Harriet began, marshalling the facts in her mind so she could tell this as succinctly as possible. 'He has speech and quite an acute mind. He remembers things he's interested in, can recite every advertising jingle ever written, looks presentable and comes across as a slightly off-beat but ordinary individual.'

She paused long enough for him to comment but his silence eventually prompted her to continue.

'As a child he was a loner but rarely in serious trouble. He was hyperactive and has a lot of repetitive behaviour that can be aggravating but, growing up in such a small community, everyone knew him and understood and the village protected him.'

'Still are, if you're leading up to telling me it was this son who beat his mother.'

His words were so crisp and condemnatory she shivered, but he didn't know it all so couldn't possibly understand.

'They do whatever they can to protect Mary as well,' Harriet protested. 'I know it's wrong and reportable and, yes, he could possibly kill her one day, but you need to see the whole picture, James, before you pass your high and mighty judgement.'

'So tell me!'

She shook her head, wishing she could get angry with him but only feeling more overwhelmed than usual by Mary's problems.

'I can't talk *and* drive,' she told him. 'Not about this. There's a track ahead that leads up to the summit. I'll pull off and we can stop there while I explain.'

James stared at her, unable to believe she'd admit to being unable to do anything! He saw the faint colour in her cheeks and knew she'd guessed his reaction, and suddenly all the anger she'd generated earlier drained away, replaced by a far more dangerous and insidious rush of desire.

She stopped the car and turned off the engine and he was surprised by the panoramic view spread beneath them. Behind them the coloured houses of Hillview were like a jigsaw pattern, while ahead he could see the top of the dark tunnel of trees leading into Gold Creek, the camping ground and a few of the scattered houses. Beyond the village serried ranks of hills marched towards the horizon, their crests a startling gold as the last rays of the sun seemed to shine more brightly in its dying flourish.

'Will had a late start to puberty, not beginning to mature until he was sixteen. Unfortunately, the hormonal changes also altered his moods. He had always been on drugs of various kinds to calm him down but when his hormones kicked in it was hard to keep them balanced. He started becoming aggressive, not all the time but when things went wrong he boiled over.'

James listened to what sounded like excuses, and the frustration he'd felt earlier returned.

'And did no one think of counselling both the boy and his parents? Were other drugs considered? He was reaching adulthood—did anyone think he might prefer to live with someone other than his mother? Non-disabled kids leave home and all the studies show that people with disabilities can live with varying levels of support in the community.'

She turned and he watched as the condemnation in her eyes turned to acceptance. Clenching her fingers on the steering-wheel, she began again.

'Yes, various people tried to help. Eventually the government appointed a doctor to do sessions out here. He wasn't drug-addicted but he was totally uncaring about anything other than getting his money at the end of each fortnight. He told Mary that Will would be better off among his peers and contacted every government department he could find. The upshot was that Will was sent down to the city to live, as you say, in the community.'

He watched her shoulders lift in a sigh, then she ran her fingers through her hair and he remembered how soft it had felt when he'd kissed her and a curl had brushed his cheek. Again the anger faded and he wanted to hold her, to share at least some of the burden of care for these people she carried so willingly.

'Didn't work?' he asked.

She must have heard the sympathy in his voice for she turned his way again, her eyes startled, her lips slightly open as she tried a little smile.

'This is his community,' she pointed out. 'Going to a city from places like Gold Creek and Hillview is confusing enough for young people with all their faculties intact—I did it so I know. For Will it was an unmitigated disaster. He was put in a house with three other young people, two of whom were also autistic. They all needed their own private space and there was none. The support workers were kind, but kindness wasn't enough. Will's rages increased and the solution was drugs. Mary saved her pension and went down once a month, and then on one visit she found him so zonked out he barely recognised her.'

James heard the quaver in Harriet's voice and took

her hand, holding it so he could rub his thumb gently over her palm as she continued her tale.

'Mary brought him home. She wrote and explained what she'd done and why, but it didn't stop the appropriate departments investigating and eventually instituting legal procedures against her, claiming Will was now eighteen and an adult and entitled to make his own decisions or have a properly appointed legal adviser make them for him. Mary was devastated.'

Harriet paused, the touch of James's thumb so distracting she could barely think straight.

'She must have battled through the red tape eventually,' he said. 'Will's obviously at home if he's the one responsible for her injuries.'

'We all got behind her. Doug had set up his practice by then and I was back from studying. Even the local farmers and graziers, who usually ignore the village politics and happenings, chipped in to fight the government.'

'And you won?' he said, and she turned and looked into his eyes, dark shadows now the sun had disappeared.

'Did we?' she queried. 'You saw yourself what happens from time to time. Mary swears she prefers putting up with Will's occasional tantrums but every time it happens I have to ask myself if she wouldn't have been better off if he'd stayed in the city. Maybe he'd have grown used to it, maybe she'd have forgotten about him.'

'A mother forget her child? It's not very likely, is it?' he asked, and Harriet felt the tears build up in her eyes then slide slowly down her cheeks.

James watched her swipe at them with her free hand, making dark smudges where dust turned to mud. He remembered the conversation she'd had with the two unsavoury youths and wondered how he could have been so insensitive as to mention mothers.

Before he could make amends she tugged her hand away from his and stared out through the windscreen.

'We've identified many trigger points that upset Will and have psychiatric reports that are very positive. Experts feel these incidents will diminish as he grows older. In fact, I think this is the first for six months. It isn't personal—he doesn't attack Mary—but he slams furniture into walls and windows and if she gets in the way, trying to stop him hurting himself, then she gets hit as well.'

She swung back to face him and hurried on, as if afraid he'd argue again when the full horror of her statement hit him. 'I know it's wrong, we all know that, but Mary's adamant he should stay at home and she's also determined he should have some quality of life so increasing his drug dosage isn't an option. All we can do is try to make it as safe as possible for her.'

There was another pause, a hesitation that James could feel as a tension in the air. He considered Mary Ogilvie's options, thought of the frail, aging woman trying to stop her son's destruction, and wondered if he'd have had the strength to make the decision she had.

'How?' he asked, realising that Harriet had decided she'd said enough and was now gazing out of the window, as if the darkening scene held some secrets she needed to know.

Slowly turning to face him again, she gave the little shrug he now recognised as part of her body language. Don't judge me harshly, it seemed to say, a contradictory gesture in one who appeared so competent.

'Will's terrified of guns and both of Mary's neighbours keep old rifles with the firing mechanisms disabled. They can bring them into the house to subdue him if they hear a commotion. I phoned Phil, one neighbour, just before we left. Unfortunately, she'd walked up the road to meet her kids off the school bus when it started and old Ernie, who lives on the other side of

Ogilvies, was down fishing at the river and didn't hear it until after Mary had tried to stop him.'

James stared at her, unable to believe what she was telling him.

'They walk into the house and point a rifle at the man?'

The smile fluttered for a moment then she sobered up and said, 'Well, they don't actually point it at him. They only have to carry it in and he stops as soon as he sees it.'

After another hesitation, this one so long that James wondered if he should speak, she added, 'Actually, it's quite, quite horrible and Mary is usually more upset about what happens afterwards than about the beating. Will breaks down completely. He curls up in a ball and sobs and cries and retreats into himself for days and days.'

How could people live this way, James wondered, with such overwhelming sadness and despair in their lives, and the death of one of them the only escape?

'So using the rifle as a deterrent to prevent the rages isn't an option,' he said slowly, and won a full-fledged smile of approval from Harriet.

'No!' she agreed. 'But it isn't all doom and gloom, remember. Will fishes and he collects rocks and he has a very happy life in between times. It's just lousy that someone who must have suffered so much mental anguish as Mary has in her life should now have to suffer physically because of her determination to let Will live as and where he wants.'

'And Mr Ogilvie?' James asked, wondering why there wasn't a man around to share Mary's burden.

'Upped and left when Will was two. Couldn't cope with a son who wasn't normal—whatever that may be.'

There was no condemnation in her voice, just a sad acceptance of the things that happened in people's lives.

James wanted to hold and comfort Harriet but he knew that it wasn't an option either.

His accident, his lengthy convalescence, Rosemary's departure from his life and his subsequent anger and bitterness had all combined to lead to a prolonged period of abstinence. Now his body had obviously recovered enough to be feeling sexual interest again and from the way it was behaving in Harriet's presence comfort would soon give way to seduction, and Harriet Logan was too nice a person to seduce.

'Well, now we've dealt with the drama of the day, we'd better go home,' she said briskly as the stars began to appear in the purple night sky. 'If I find some steak, will you chuck it on the barbecue while I make us a salad?' She had started the engine and was turning to head back down the track when she spoke, but her voice was strained.

They drove in silence, Harriet still fighting the unexpected regret that had enveloped her when James had spoken of a mother's love for her child. On Sunday evening she'd talked of layers of self, perhaps because she'd subconsciously realised that hers were being gradually eroded and the only explanation for her sudden bouts of vulnerability was this man's presence in her life.

As if she'd prompted him, he asked the question. 'How did your family come to Gold Creek?'

She stared at him, then realised it was a normal, getting-to-know-you question and not some transposition of her thoughts to him.

'My great-grandfather was a dreamer,' she said lightly, finding solace in a story she'd repeated many times before. 'And he had the fever, as they still call it around here. Gold fever. He dragged his wife to every new strike, every new gold field, from Victoria to here. When they reached Gold Creek she was pregnant with her second child and she decided enough was enough.'

Harriet turned into her street and drew up outside her house.

'When my great-grandfather heard of gold further north she refused to move and he took off.' She turned to face James. 'My family seems to have two kinds of people, the nomads and the stay-at-homes. My great-grandmother became a stay-at-home. She had a small bark hut but she made do and took in boarders and did washing. When the second strike brought hundreds more miners to the area she borrowed money—unheard-of for a woman in those days—and built a fine hotel.'

'This house?' James asked, looking towards the old building.

'This very house,' Harriet assured him. 'It's why I bought it,' she added. 'I'm another of the stay-at-homes.'

He looked at her, as if assessing the meaning of her words, but there was too much emotion trapped in the air between them and she jumped down from the car, took the steps in one stride and entered the house. Quite forgetting that it was no longer a refuge but just a larger cage she had to share with the man who was not only affecting the workings of her body in an undeniably sexual way but was also cracking her defences, exposing the soft, unprotected bits of Harriet Logan.

'I'll have a shower then come down and see to dinner,' she said when she heard him cross the verandah behind her.

'Harriet!' he began, but she hurried on up the stairs, pretending she hadn't heard him.

By the time she came back down her mind was back in practical mode, fixed firmly on preparing a meal for the two of them—until she saw James in the kitchen, bent over the grained timber chopping board with an apron tucked around his waist, one long, lean hand grasping a carving knife as he sliced tomatoes with swift, sure strokes.

'Beat you to it,' he said, glancing up and smiling as

she approached. 'You do the driving so it's time I took on more of the cooking. I'm going to do both the salad and the steak and I want you to sit down and relax. I've a bottle of white wine opened in the refrigerator—a local product purchased last weekend. It's very good, will you try a glass?'

Harriet eyed him suspiciously. That was probably the longest string of sentences she'd ever heard from him—not personal, of course, but still a lot of words. Was he covering up—hiding something?

'Is your leg hurting?' she demanded, and was startled by his answering shout of laughter.

'Suspicious creature!' he chided. 'Can't I offer you a drink simply as a courtesy?'

No, she thought but she didn't say it, crossing instead to the refrigerator and pulling out the bottle of wine. It was a 1995 Chardonnay, local, as he'd said, but she knew enough about the local wineries to know it had won several medals at major shows.

She poured herself a glass, replaced the bottle and looked around the room, wondering what to do next and why she should feel uncomfortable in her own kitchen.

'Go and sit outside,' he suggested. 'I'll be finished here in a couple of minutes and will throw on the steaks and you can watch a real expert at work.'

'Too domestic to be true, this scene,' she mumbled to herself as she walked obediently outside. The only trouble was that his domesticity didn't detract one iota from his sexuality. In fact, she doubted she'd ever meet a man who would look better in her lilac gingham apron. She pictured him in just the gingham apron and pressed the wine glass to her rapidly heating cheeks.

Perhaps she simply needed the physical release of sex. She'd fallen in love with a fellow student when she was studying and had enjoyed the sexual side of their relationship, but love had cooled to friendship and she'd had no regrets when they'd parted.

But, surely, if it was as simple as her body's need for sex she could have gone to bed with Doug ages ago. True, he hadn't pressed her but nor had she encouraged intimacies, preferring to keep their friendship on a more platonic basis. No, sex was something she hadn't given much thought to for years—and had given too much to this last week!

'Worth a penny, those thoughts?'

She turned at the sound of his voice and saw him coming out of the kitchen. A fiery heat told her she was blushing again.

'Not even a cent,' she declared. 'But I feel useless, sitting here. Isn't there something I can do?'

He paused by the barbecue, and looked from the lid to the tray in his hands, then across towards her.

'You can come and hold the tray for me,' he said. 'You should have a little table over here for putting things on.'

She put down her wine and walked across to take the tray. 'I do have a little table but I took it upstairs so I could stand on it when I was painting. I—'

One touch of his fingers was enough to stop her breath. One accidental brush of hand on hand beneath the tray.

'You?' he murmured, his hands holding hers now yet still supporting the tray between them, his eyes fixed on her lips as he leaned towards her. In the second before their lips met he muttered, 'Weird!' Harriet heard the sentiment echoed in her mind as she kissed him back, delighting in the taste of wine upon his lips and the lingering tang of toothpaste when his tongue invaded her mouth.

CHAPTER NINE

IT WAS more than weird, Harriet realised as James took the tray from her hands, set it on the larger table while he carried a chair across towards the barbecue and then retrieved the tray and rested it on the chair.

She watched his movements, neat and capable, and wondered why she couldn't set those tantalising kisses aside as easily.

'You get the wine and the salad,' he suggested. 'Two glasses in an evening shouldn't render us incapable of helping anyone who needs our help.'

But who's going to help me? Harriet thought.

Doug! she decided as the phone rang, and she hurried into the hall to answer it.

He was full of news of his fellow competitors, dutifully concerned about Maud, joked about James's acceptance in the community, asked automatically if she'd changed her mind and then returned to what he'd rung for—to regale her with the tale of his triumphs at the halfway stage of the contest.

No, neither thoughts of Doug nor Doug in person would save her from her feelings for James Hepworth. She only half listened to the rest of what he was saying, puzzled for a moment when he claimed this was the last time he was going to ask her to marry him. She said no again, hung up, found the wine and headed back outside.

'I might have two more glasses,' she told him, 'and let you take the calls.'

'Let me drive your precious vehicle?' The mocking disbelief in his voice made her smile and she realised how often she found herself smiling in this man's company. Yet surely she'd never been short on smiles before he came?

She poured herself a glass of wine, remembering James's complaint that she was too cheerful that first day.

'Do I still strike you as a cheerful person?'

He turned from the barbecue and studied her, as if the answer might be revealed in her appearance.

'Cheerful sounds too forced,' he teased. 'You must have had some of those brisk, ever-smiling-and-how-are-we-today sisters on the wards when you were training.'

She shuddered in horror at the image.

'I know you call me Sister Bossy, but tell me I'm not like that,' she pleaded, and was rewarded with a smile that started shut-down in her breathing and melt-down in her bones.

'You're exactly like that,' he told her, 'but only when you need to be. At other times you let that image slip and you're not afraid to show people that you care about them, no matter how big or small their problem might be. You showed that by spending the night with Kate when Shaun had his triple antigen, and in a dozen other ways since then.'

Disconcerted by his praise, she sipped at her wine. 'They're my friends as well as patients,' she reminded him.

'The lad who was going off to find his father was a total stranger,' he said, then he turned back to the bar-becue and prodded the steak with the tines of the fork. 'He worries me. I suppose talking about Will has brought him back to mind. At least Will has a loving, caring mother who will always fight to see he's happy.' He put the steaks on to plates and carried them to the table.

'But what of that other young man, he and all the young people like him who have never had the oppor-tunities of knowing normal family life, of growing up with the knowledge that someone valued them? They're left to fend for themselves without the skills they need to form relationships with other people.'

Harriet tried the steak as she considered his words.

'That someone valued them,' she repeated. 'Yes, that's the important part. I can see that now!'

He cocked his head, asking the question.

'Pop, my grandfather, brought me up, but you're right—I made it through because he valued me.' She felt the lump in her throat and swallowed hard.

'So, in spite of being abandoned by your mother, you pulled through.'

The word 'abandoned' shivered in Harriet's heart like a fine sliver of glass but she smiled as she said, 'Pop thought I was wonderful and, of course, I believed him. Why shouldn't I?'

'Why shouldn't you, indeed?' Gleaming eyes teased her. 'But you see what I mean about being valued.'

With considerable difficulty Harriet switched her thoughts from gleaming eyes to his conversation.

'Are you sure it was surgery you intended to pursue? Your thoughts lead back to psychiatry on a regular basis. If you're not analysing me you're puzzling over someone else's behaviour.'

He grinned at her.

'Not behaviour so much as futures this time,' he argued. 'I did consider psychiatry as a specialty but I told myself it was unproductive in that you could help people see what was wrong in their lives but once they walked out the door you had no power over what happened to them.'

'Having power over people's lives is dangerous,' Harriet reminded him. 'Isn't psychiatry all about giving people power over their own lives?'

'Of course it is,' he replied, leaning forward as he made his point, his meal forgotten in the force of his persuasion. 'But what power, what control, can they have when there's nothing out there for them, when they have no hope for the future? All new self-awareness can do is emphasise what isn't going right for them.'

'But how can that be altered?' Harriet asked him, touched by this concern in a man she would once have judged to be immune to others' sorrows.

'That's the question, Harriet. That's the question!'

He turned his attention back to his meal, eating with the same concentration he'd given to their conversation—and, earlier, to the kiss.

They talked desultorily, discussing patients and how she coped during the Christmas holiday time when the tourist season was at its busiest but the doctor's visits stopped for a month. Yet Harriet sensed James was merely filling in time, responding mechanically while his mind raced along other tracks. She cleared the table and he followed her into the kitchen.

'Of course, you'll never save everyone and the few you could help would be a pitiful percentage of the whole, but would it be worth trying for the few?'

Harriet stared at him. 'OK,' she admitted. 'You've lost me.'

He looked startled for a moment, then he smiled and touched her shoulder.

'I'm sorry,' he said. 'I've been thinking about the future.'

'So I noticed,' she said kindly, removing the teatowel from his hand before he could use it to dry an unwashed plate.

He chuckled and his fingers tightened momentarily on her arm.

'Well, it's safer than thinking about sex,' he admitted, 'which I'm beginning to find in my mind quite regularly these days.'

The heat began in the region of her breasts and was creeping up her neck when he released her arm, touched her cheek and murmured, 'Don't you agree?'

'Definitely!' she managed to stammer, the word strangling her tonsils and twisting her tongue.

'And now I need reassurance, I suppose, that even one life saved from almost certain disaster is better than none. Or would you hold to the theory that we're better to put Band-Aids on the lot and hope the problem will eventually go away?'

She stared at him, lost in a welter of thought and emotion.

'Go into the sitting room and do your thinking there,' she ordered. 'Now!' she added when he showed no sign of moving. 'I'll clean up and come and join you. Just try to sort all these mighty thoughts of yours into the kind of order a simple nursing sister can understand.'

He hesitated a fraction longer then he flicked her cheek with his finger once again and left, but his words floated back to her.

'A simple nursing sister? I don't think!'

By the time she carried their coffee into the front room he had pieces of paper spread out over every flat surface, with diagrams and notes written in his bold handwriting.

'What is all of this?' she demanded.

He grinned at her.

'All I can remember about self-esteem and self-worth and developing relationships and the stages of maturity. I find if I write things down more comes back to me. I'm not sure where it will lead but it seemed important to get it stirring in my brain.'

'And cluttering up my sitting room,' Harriet added, brushing three pieces of paper off the table so she could set down the coffee.

'I'm sorry,' he said, but she could see he wasn't. What he was was excited.

'It's about self-worth, isn't it, Harriet? About building that up within a person so, no matter what happens in the future, he or she will never lose that sense of self. You talked about peeling back layers, but that's where so much psychiatry fails. We leave the person vulnerable. To succeed we have to put that person back together again, and talk alone can't do that.'

Harriet heard commitment in his voice, and something else—challenge. It made James Hepworth more real—more likeable. Had the challenge of organ transplants taken precedence over this earlier interest?

'What was the real reason you opted out of psychiatry?' Harriet asked him, and saw the excitement in his face still and then fade gradually away, as if her question had turned off a switch.

He studied her for a moment and she realised he was thinking back so when he smiled, with his lips but not with his eyes, she wondered where his thoughts had led that sadness had followed them.

'Now you've made me think about it,' he said slowly, 'I realise I was probably influenced. I was in general practice at the time and thinking about specialising. Surgery was more socially acceptable, more financially rewarding, than psychiatry. The switch to organ transplants came later because that team was considered élite—the best of the best.'

'Of course, that's the only possible reason for choosing a career,' Harriet said scathingly. 'By its position on the social ladder!' She didn't bother to hide the disappointment his admission had caused her.

'At least I'm honest enough to admit it,' he retorted. 'Not all decisions in life are as clear-cut as yours apparently was.'

'Mine was not! I could have stayed in Sydney where I studied. In fact, my boyfriend wanted me to but I chose to come back here because I felt...'

'Felt you were needed, or owed it to your grandfather? Either way, there were emotional considerations, weren't there? And if either, or both combined, were stronger than your involvement with this boyfriend then he can't have meant much to you!'

James saw her flinch and knew he'd had no right to say what he had. But the mention of a boyfriend had unsettled him even more than his own private musings.

'I'm sorry, Harriet, that was way out of line!' He wanted to touch her, to show her how sorry he was, but if he touched her he'd kiss her and he didn't know how long he could stop at kisses.

She shrugged off his apology and waved her hand towards his coffee.

'I started the questions,' she admitted, 'and we seem to have drifted away from your idea.'

Could she sense the sexual tension in his body? Was that why she'd swung the subject back to psychiatry?

'Are you and Doug an item?' The words were said before he had a chance to consider them, and from look on her face nothing could have confused her more.

'An item?' she repeated. 'What kind of adolescent language is that? If you're asking if we're lovers then the answer is no, not that it's any of your business.'

She pushed her coffee-cup aside and stood, poised for imminent flight.

'Don't go!' he asked. 'I do want to talk about other things—it's just this attraction thing I feel for you keeps getting in the way.'

Harriet stared at him, unable to believe what she was hearing.

'Attraction thing!' she echoed in blistering tones. 'How inconvenient for you! And just what does it keep getting in the way of? Politeness? Common sense? Rational conversations?'

His smile made her heart skitter even more erratically than the word 'attraction' had, but she resolutely ignored it and continued to glare at him, awaiting an answer to her very ungrammatical questions.

'Everything, wouldn't you say?' His eyes glinted wickedly and she wished she'd walked away instead of staying to vent a little spleen. 'Or are you going to deny it's there, Harriet? Deny your body's needs and responses? Your own sexuality?'

'My body doesn't have needs,' she began, and saw his smile turn to a deep, soft chuckle that played across her skin like a breeze across still water.

'Want to bet?' he said, rising slowly to his feet while his eyes challenged hers to tell the lie.

'No!' she said, but it was too late because he was already touching her, drawing her closer, fitting her body to his with gentle hands that swayed her to his will.

'No!' she said again, more loudly and insistently, pushing at his shoulders while her heart beat so quickly she knew he must be feeling its frantic rhythm against his chest. 'Let's talk about psychiatry, and your ideas, and that young man.'

He released her, but before she could organise her mind to tell her legs to move away he had placed his hand across her left breast so it pressed against her overactive heart and felt the pulsing beats she couldn't control.

'Perhaps it's better,' he murmured, and brushed his other hand through her hair, teasing his fingers into her curls and tugging slightly as if testing their resilience. 'But I want you, Harriet, and I think you want me.'

He bent to kiss her, as she'd half feared, half hoped he would. But it wasn't a tempting kiss of passion, just a repetition of the 'weird' testing kisses he'd been pressing on her lips in an almost absent-minded fashion for the last few days.

'I need to think some more before I talk,' he said at last. 'And perhaps phone my mother.'

'Phone your mother?' Harriet echoed, more confused than ever, especially when he smiled and kissed her again in a casual fashion.

'It's the done thing for sons,' he whispered in her ear. 'Now go to bed before I start something we might both have trouble not finishing.'

He turned her around and gave her a little push towards the stairs.

'Goodnight, Harriet.'

She left reluctantly but whether because she'd enjoyed the excitement which had radiated from him as he'd talked of the young people society was failing or because she wanted to stay near him she couldn't decide.

A little bit of both, perhaps, and that was dangerous. She'd lived alone—except for occasional tourists who kept to themselves—for four years, and would have to again very soon. Now was not the time to be thinking she enjoyed—needed—company in the house. Lying in bed a little later, she stared out through the window, but the beauty of the night sky, the brightness of the stars and pale glow of moonlight did little to alleviate a new ache deep within her.

She woke to a fresh new day, filled with sunshine and promise. The sitting room was tidy, with no papers strewn across her furniture, and there was silence from the bedroom beyond it which suggested James had had a late night with his thoughts and ideas.

Thinking she'd leave him to sleep a little longer, she grabbed her coat off the hook in the hall and let herself quietly out of the house. She'd go down and feed Bert's hens. The walk in the cool, clean air might chase away the ghosts of sleep.

But Harriet's own particular ghost was ahead of her, standing propped against the wire of the run watching the hens squabble over their fresh feed.

'I couldn't sleep so I thought I'd save you the chore,' he said, his gaze skimming over her then settling on her eyes, as if he hoped to read some secret there. 'I intended being home in time to start our breakfast but was caught up in their behaviour.'

He slipped his arm through hers and began to walk back through the garden.

'To get anywhere with disadvantaged youth you'd need a leader,' James continued, as if their previous night's conversation had never stopped. 'Someone the others can relate to but whom they also find admirable—someone they'd consider "one of them" as against "one of us".'

She felt so warm and contented, walking with him with their arms linked and their bodies touching, that she didn't question his 'them and us' assertion but kept quiet and let him think his thoughts aloud. He was walking more easily, the nurse in her realised, and she wondered—

'Are you listening to all this drivel or wondering if you're working with a madman?'

She pulled her arm from his so she could face him.

'Half listening,' she admitted.

James smiled at that, but his eyes glowed with the excitement his thoughts had generated.

'I tend to talk my ideas through,' he apologised. 'It helps me see the weaknesses and sort things out in my head.'

'Then keep talking,' Harriet told him. 'I'm happy to listen.'

She said the words but realised they weren't one hundred per cent true. He began to speak again but her thoughts erased the words. It was her own fault, of course. She'd prodded him to think about the future, reawakened his interest in psychiatry, because she'd felt the weight of his depression over his future.

Now all his mental energy was focussed on the 'lost youth' of this generation—lost youth that inhabited cities, not small country towns. In his mind this month was already behind him and he was reaching forward again, enlivened by a great new challenge. A great new challenge she would listen to but never see him meet.

'So it's OK if my mother comes? She can have your other room?'

They'd reached home and were climbing the front steps when the questions battled through to her consciousness.

'Your mother? Here? When?'

'Saturday,' he said, and touched her lightly on the shoulder. 'Don't panic, you'll love her. She'll look after herself—look after both of us as well most probably.'

'We'd better have breakfast.' Harriet could think of nothing else to say. 'We're already running late.'

They entered the house as the phone rang—a child had croup.

'Stop panicking, Jill, it's not as bad as it sounds,' Harriet said into the phone when the noise of coughing and hysteria had dulled enough for her to be heard. 'Go into the bathroom, close the door and turn on the hot water from the shower. Stay in the steam until I get there.'

She turned to James. 'I'll go, you eat then head down to the surgery. I hope you're not overdoing the walking,' she added anxiously, although she no longer argued with his decision to walk to and from work.

'What will you do?' he asked as she quickly checked the contents of her bag.

'Soothe the anxiety and if the steam has reduced the spasm of his laryngeal muscles I'll suggest a restful day and warn Jill it could recur at night. She can come down later and pick up a humidifier from the surgery and put it in his room tonight. He's two years old and it hasn't happened before so I guess it's the sudden change in temperature that's done it.'

'You're a damn good nurse, Sister Logan,' James said softly, then he drew her into his arms and kissed her quickly on the lips, but whether he was kissing the nurse or the person she was left to wonder as she drove towards the home of the sick child.

By the time she arrived the harsh coughing had diminished and the child's breathing seemed easy and relaxed, although Harriet detected a slight whistling noise on inspiration and advised the mother to stay in the steam-filled room a little longer.

'Then change him into dry clothes and tuck him into bed. He'll sleep because the panic caused by his not being able to breathe is very debilitating.'

As she spoke she noticed the little head settling more easily against his mother's breast and the almost translucent eyelids dropping closed.

'He's asleep now,' Jill said softly, then she looked up at Harriet, her eyes sheened by tears. 'Thanks for coming. John's away with his work and I was on my own. I went mental.'

'Why wouldn't you?' Harriet said, bending to kiss the baby on the cheek.

She drove home for a quick cup of coffee and a piece of toast, then went on to the surgery, with kisses, not babies, now on her mind. She had to stop James kissing her, that was the first thing she had to do. She was finding his kisses more and more addictive but in a little over a fortnight he'd be gone and she'd be left to fight the demons of withdrawal on her own.

You could go with him, the woman, not the nurse, suggested. Or, if not with him, relocate so you were at least in the same city. Give yourself a chance!

She pulled up outside the old building and thought of city clinics she'd seen, shiny new buildings, all chrome and marble inside, with state-of-the-art technology to help diagnoses and doctors available twenty-four hours a day to back up a nurse's judgement.

'Hey, Harry, you're already late. Whatcha doing dreaming out there?'

It was Jack Gibbes, their resident poet, a down-to-earth bushman who wrote verses that reached into the hearts and souls of country folk, revealing their pain as well as their triumphs.

'I'm contemplating a future in a place where no one

calls me Harry,' she said with a sardonic grin. 'Wouldn't anonymity be nice?'

'You couldn't leave Gold Creek, girl,' Jack told her, putting his arm around her shoulder as she reached the stairs and giving her a warm hug. 'Your roots go down too deep.'

It was hard to hear her thoughts put into words—unacceptably hard. She pushed herself away from Jack and said, 'Nonsense, I'm tough, I could transplant to anywhere.'

Jack followed her up the stairs.

'But your roots are tangled up with other people's, Harry. Pulling yours up would damage theirs.'

'Why should I care?' she demanded, swinging around to face this man who was hammering at her with truths she didn't want to hear.

'You two chased all the patients away with your argument?'

Harriet felt her shoulders slump. She turned back towards the waiting room and saw James standing at the inner door.

'You've no patients?' she demanded, changing the subject as quickly as she could. 'Where's Marj?'

He waved his hand towards the empty desk. 'You tell me, I just work here!'

Harriet swung back to Jack.

'Are you here for an appointment? Do you know what's happening?'

He smiled at her as if he'd won the unfinished argument, then addressed himself to James.

'Jack Gibbes!' he said. 'Actually, I was coming down to give you a message from Marj. She's running late and asked me to fill in for her as I'm not busy.'

Harriet hid a smile as James looked slightly taken aback by this offer. He probably didn't get many men in tattered blue overalls coming to fill in for his receptionist.

'In fact,' Jack continued, 'as you've got no customers, why don't you take the new doc for a drive out to Pop's lease, Harriet? Take that dandy little go-anywhere phone with you and I'll give you a call when folk begin to arrive.'

'Harriet?' James looked at her, waiting for her either to agree to or veto this suggestion.

'Do you want to go for a drive?' she asked, half eager, half dreading it. 'I suppose you haven't seen much of the place, apart from the roads in and out.'

'I'd like it,' he said, and nodded to Jack. 'That's if you don't mind manning the phone and keeping the hordes under control.'

Jack grinned in reply and waved them towards the door. 'Just lock up inside before you go,' he said. 'I don't want to be responsible for your gear.'

Feeling slightly guilty at being free on a working day, Harriet waited while James locked up. As they drove up the street towards the hotel she saw the queue reaching from the corner beyond it down the footpath almost to her house.

'Of course, it's a third Wednesday!' she muttered to herself.

'Third Wednesday?' James repeated, staring out at the happy, chattering people who stood and waited in line. 'Does someone come to town, giving away money? I can't think why else the entire population would line the street like this.'

Harriet waved to friends and continued, turning left out of town where the dark cypresses began.

'It's the fisho,' she explained.

'Fisho?' James repeated, as if he was having trouble understanding her words.

'Fishmonger!' she elaborated. 'This is the country. No fresh salt-water fish or prawns or any other seafood, except every third Wednesday in the month when the fisho comes to town.'

'And those people line up like that and wait for him? There are dozens of them there.'

Harriet chuckled as she turned to him.

'Puts you right back in your place, doesn't it?' she teased. 'You've no patients because the fisho is far more important.'

He laughed and her heart responded to the sound, but Jack's words still lingered in her head and a sadness that had nothing to do with driving out to Pop's old lease began to settle in her stomach like an undigested meal.

'This country's beautiful,' James said, 'softer and less stark than the Hillview side of town.'

'Tableland country,' Harriet told him, turning off onto an even narrower dirt road winding back down towards the creek. 'It was a farmer, herding sheep, who found the first gold in this area, and farming has provided the district with more long-term stability than gold, although that's changing these days as the young kids head for town, unwilling to settle for a life in the bush.'

'I wonder, then, if kids who have no life in the city would settle for one in the country,' James mused, but before Harriet could question his train of thought she saw a movement in the bushes at the side of the road.

She stopped the car and jumped out, jogging back to where she thought she'd seen—

It was there, a joey, furred but still too young to survive alone out of its mother's pouch.

'What is it? What's wrong?' James called as he came hurrying awkwardly towards her.

Harriet pulled off her sweater and bundled the little animal into it, her eyes searching the area for a sign of the adult kangaroo.

'Shooters!' she said scathingly as James reached out to touch the silky head that peered out from the warm folds of wool. 'I know there are places where kangaroos compete with sheep or cattle for little available grass and where controlled culling is necessary, but we've no problem here and the abundance of wildlife is part of what attracts tourists to the area.'

'Mightn't the mother return?' James asked. Harriet shook her head and held the little creature with its comically long ears and huge frightened eyes a little closer to her breast.

'A doe will tip a baby out of her pouch and hide him in long grass or bushes when she senses danger, but she'd have been back to collect him as soon as the danger passed—if she was alive.'

She headed slowly back towards the Jeep, waited until James had climbed in and then she handed her precious bundle to him.

'You'll have to hold him while I drive,' she said.

'You checked on his sex?' he asked, making her smile at the mock horror in his voice.

'No, but he looks like a he, don't you think?' She walked around the bonnet to climb in beside him and was surprised to see the soft tenderness on his face as he studied his new charge.

'He is a boy,' he announced as she drove slowly along the narrow road, searching for a sign of the mother. 'What shall we call him?'

Momentarily diverted, she glanced at him and smiled. 'I think the father should choose the boys' names, don't you, and leave the girls' for the mother?'

He met her eyes, his asking questions, and she was sorry she'd turned the conversation from purely practical to what was almost romantic nonsense.

'Walter would be nice,' he said gravely, and she relaxed again. He hadn't taken it personally after all.

'Walter!' she repeated. 'Yes, he should be proud of a fine, upstanding name like that.'

CHAPTER TEN

JAMES felt the little animal move on his lap, finally settling into what seemed a most uncomfortable position
with his elongated toes and his strong tail curled up near
his face.

'They travel like that in the mother's pouch,' Harriet
said as she turned off the road, across a cattle grid and
drew up beside an old timber shanty. 'This is where I
grew up,' she added, as if the two things were connected.

James looked around, surprised by both the beauty of
the surrounding hills and the apparent poverty of the
only dwelling.

'It was my great-grandmother's house,' she added,
and grinned. 'But I guess you didn't need to be told that.
Come and have a look.'

She leapt out of the car and walked off, and he sensed
she might need time alone.

'And what of you?' James asked the sleeping Walter.
'Do I leave you here or would you like to tag along?'

Deciding that the animal probably needed the warmth
it was drawing from his body, he guessed he should take
it along, but clambering out of the Jeep with a bad leg
and no hands to support himself wasn't an option. He
was considering ways and means when Harriet reappeared, a jute bag in her hands.

'Here,' she called. 'I'll make him a pouch with this.'

Back at the car she opened her emergency bag and
found a pair of scissors. Using these, she cut a slit across
one side of the bag, about halfway down.

'Now I'll hang the bag over the back of the car seat,'

she explained, 'and pop him in. He'll think he's home again.'

'Except there's no comforting milky teat to latch onto in the bag.'

Harriet threw him a look that told him she hadn't realised he knew much about kangaroos, then she nodded.

'Yes, I think he's young enough to have still been on the teat, but the season is good and Mum might have decided it was time to have another one so there could already have been a little usurper latched on in his place.'

'Amazing creatures,' James agreed, handing her the bundled joey and watching as she eased him, sweater and all, into the now hanging bag. 'Fancy being able to hold back embryonic young until nature produced the kind of weather patterns that would give the new offspring the best chance of survival.'

'Perhaps it's something humans should develop instead of willy-nilly pregnancies which result in unwanted children.'

James tested the words for bitterness as he watched her straighten, but decided it wasn't there. Regret, perhaps, and understanding of the dilemma facing the human race when pressures of daily life made it impossible for some people to cope with the problems and responsibilities parenthood imposed.

'Maybe more emphasis should be placed on parenting skills in schools,' he said slowly, once again talking his way through a thought. 'More dialogue with teenagers about the gaps between perception and reality, particularly with regard to relationships and children.'

Harriet nodded her agreement and he felt a rush of warmth that he could share these first tentative forays towards a possible future with someone so unjudgemental.

'Well, this is it,' she said, diverting him from possible futures to the present.

He looked at 'it' and was surprised to find that, front on, the house was much bigger than it had seemed.

'She started with just this bit,' Harriet explained, leading him across a shaded strip of packed dirt and into the dim interior of the place. 'Slab walls lined with bags or paper, held in place by a kind of slurry mixed up from the clay down at the creek.'

His eyes adjusted and he saw the old stone fireplace set in the back wall, with an iron bar across it and an ancient kettle still hanging from a hook above where the fire would be. In front of it stood a solid timber table and four chairs, unpainted but sturdy and honest in their construction. Against the side wall an old dresser with patterned glass set into the top cupboard doors took James back in memory to his childhood and his grandmother's house. He felt a sense of comfort and belonging.

'Pop said they had a curtain that divided off this bit,' Harriet told him, gesturing to an area about the size of a large bed. 'It hid the family's bed from the kitchen where Great-Grandma fed the boarders.'

Harriet hesitated as the atmosphere in the room seemed to thicken..She was sorry she'd mentioned beds.

'And she built on more rooms for the boarders?' James asked.

'Yes, come and look,' she said, pleased to have an excuse to move out of the shadows.

Not that the other rooms were much brighter.

'They all open off the verandah, and out the back there's a shower room under the old tank-stand,' she explained, leading James first into what had been her room when she was growing up. She tried to see it through his eyes but couldn't imagine what he'd make of the pictures of flowers and babies she'd pasted on the walls in her childhood, of the horses which had been her teenage passion, and the postcards she'd sent from Sydney when she'd gone off to the big city and been constantly surprised and bemused by the buildings and people!

'I'm glad you managed to see all the sights,' he said, moving towards the postcard collection and studying the places as if he was interested in where she'd been.

'It's a huge culture shock to a country kid,' she explained, moving closer to recall the moments in the pictures.

He put his arm around her casually, as Doug did from time to time.

'Did you enjoy the city?' he asked.

She shrugged. 'It's different,' she admitted. 'The people all seem to move faster, to speak more quickly, to be busier than country folk—their doings more important somehow.'

'And was Jack right or wrong when he talked about your roots? Would you transplant?'

Harriet moved away from him so he couldn't feel her doubts, and confirmed what she'd said earlier.

'I'm tough, I'd transplant.'

He reached out and took her chin, tilting her head so he could look into her eyes.

'And not be bothered, not have regrets, about the other roots you might disturb.'

She twisted out of his grasp and glared at him.

'Jack's a poet,' she said scathingly. 'That's just the kind of poetic flight of fantasy he loves to indulge in. He says the words aloud to see if he can use them in his work some time. They don't mean anything.' She walked away from him.

'Don't they?' His quiet question followed her and she wondered why he was asking, why he cared about whether or not she could dig up her roots and move on to another place, another life.

As she pushed open the door to the next room— Grandma's room in her mind, although Grandma had died many years before Pop and he'd continued to sleep in it—James caught up with her. He put his hands on her shoulders and drew her back against his body.

She tried to move away but her momentum only made it easier for him to turn her in his arms, and this time he held her as he kissed her, seeming to taste her first as he always did with those light brushes of lips on lips. But then he groaned and drew her closer and there was nothing weird about the passion that flared between them.

It was as wild as the wind through the trees in winter, filling her body with fierce flames that licked along the hidden pathways of desire, setting alight everything they touched.

It's just a kiss, she told herself, but 'just a kiss' didn't begin to describe it. Nor explain the sensations that 'just a kiss' had caused.

'We've got to get back,' she said unevenly when his exploring hands had reduced her bones to jelly and it was all she could do to prevent herself dragging him across the room to Grandma's old brass bed. 'The fisho—'

'The fisho?' His head shot up and he peered down at her, his eyes glazed by the same desire she'd felt. 'I'm trying to seduce you and you're thinking of fish.'

Harriet felt a smile wobble on her lips.

'Not thinking of fish so much as patients,' she explained. Then she had to ask. 'Were you really trying to seduce me?'

James looked into the blue eyes that stared so frankly up at him. Eyes you could drown in, he realised. But there were shadows in those blue depths, an uncertainty he found strange but poignant in someone so capable and managing.

'Or you were seducing me,' he teased, to chase away the shadows and make her tentative smile more secure. 'So, whether it's fish or patients, we'd better go back to town.'

The smile settled back into place but she hesitated, before nodding, and he found himself thinking that it wouldn't take much persuasion to make her forget her duty for a while longer.

'May I bring my mother out here?' he asked as they walked back to the car.

She seemed surprised but her smile widened and finally reached her eyes.

'Of course,' she said. 'She might like to try a little gold-panning in the creek. We can make a picnic of it on Sunday if you like...'

The words disappeared into nothingness and he saw the smile had slipped a little. He scanned back through the conversation and guessed at her sudden withdrawal.

'Hey,' he said, catching up with her and taking her hand. 'I have no great desire to be alone with my mother and I'm sure she has none to be alone with me. We'll make a picnic of it, as you say—the three of us. Something to look forward to, and you'll have the security of knowing there's a chaperone to save you being tumbled on that old bed.'

He heard her chuckle and almost sighed with relief, although why making Harriet feel comfortable should be important to him he couldn't fathom.

Something to look forward to! Harriet thought, checking her new charge before climbing into the car. She glanced at James and saw him smile, and wondered if love had the same symptoms as the beginning of a viral complaint—a slightly queasy stomach and an internal uneasiness that was hard to define. Maybe she needed a second opinion...

They were crossing the grid when the phone rang. 'Now that could have proved untimely,' James murmured as he lifted it to answer.

Harriet felt the heat crawl into her cheeks, doubling in intensity when Jack's voice said clearly, 'Hope I'm not interrupting anything but you've four patients waiting.'

'We're on our way,' James told him, then turned to Harriet and held up five fingers.

She nodded and listened while he told Jack they'd be there in five minutes then asked for any other messages.

'One or two. I've got them written down, there's nothing urgent,' Jack said.

James ended the call. 'Is there a confidentiality issue involved with Jack being in Marj's place?' he asked.

Harriet found herself smiling again. 'There's a confidentiality issue about living in a small country community,' she replied. 'Everyone knows everyone else's business anyway. Jack often does our reception work so he knows not to talk, and patients won't tell him anything they're not comfortable about him knowing.'

She watched James out of the corner of her eye, marvelling at his thirst for information—at the way he seemed to absorb it so effortlessly. Then his profile came into focus and she was admiring it—

'Hey, you missed the house,' he said suddenly, and she wondered if absent-mindedness was another symptom of love.

There was no time for absent-mindedness once they entered the building. The late start meant they were busy until the sun began to set behind the hills.

'Any house calls?' James asked when his last patient had departed. He was standing in the doorway to the kitchen, watching Harriet pick grains of gravel out of a bad graze on a child's leg. He noticed the bag hanging over the back of Harriet's chair and realised he'd forgotten about the new member of their small household.

'Two,' she told him. 'Your favourite patient, Mrs Reynolds, is one. Janet's concerned because she's coughing a lot.' They exchanged a glance that told him she suspected, as he did, that it could be congestive heart failure.

'At her age you have to expect it,' he said quietly, and Harriet nodded her agreement.

'The second call is at the pub,' she told him. 'Betty Pearce phoned. She's worried about Kate. Evidently she's not sleeping well, not eating—nothing wrong, she says, but Betty's concerned about her because she seems to have no energy and has taken to her bed.'

'And your diagnosis?' he asked, and she started in surprise and caught the smile lurking in his eyes.

'Check for swollen glands and blood test for glandular fever,' she told him promptly. 'Kate's back at school—her mother minds Shaun during the day. It's the most likely explanation for general lassitude with no real symptoms at Kate's age.'

James watched her bend over the child's leg again and continue the painstaking work.

'Do you trust me to go off and do these visits on my own?' he asked. 'You're going to be busy there for a while.'

'Oh, would you?' she asked, looking up again and flashing him a grateful smile. 'Take the Jeep, I'll walk home. Actually, if you're going to be at the pub you might like to eat there. I've a hell of a lot of paperwork to catch up on here so I'll eat the sandwiches we didn't eat for lunch and stay on to get it done.'

He studied her for a moment, uncertain enough to wonder if she was making work an excuse to avoid him.

'OK!' he said quietly, but the thought nagged in his mind as he headed for Mrs Reynolds'.

Not that he could blame her. He'd been monopolising her free time since his arrival, which might be difficult for someone as independent as he believed Harriet to be. Perhaps she just needed some time alone.

Or maybe it had been his talk of seduction that had frightened her. Heaven knew why he'd said that when Harriet Logan was the last person he should be seducing.

By eleven he'd decided she'd had more than enough

time alone and was about to drive down to the clinic and collect her when he heard her footsteps on the verandah. He stood but hadn't made it to the front door by the time she entered, her arms full of jute bag and joey, her face white with weariness.

'I shouldn't have left you there without transport,' he scolded, taking the joey from her and following her towards the kitchen.

'I was fine, and the walk is always pleasant,' she told him, filling the kettle and setting it to boil. 'I wouldn't have been this late but I let Walter out for a hop in the back yard down there, then couldn't find him. I think he's older than he looks because he seemed to understand grass is for eating.'

'And how old are they when they start doing that?' James asked, a little put out to find it had been Walter, not seduction, on her mind all the time.

'Eight or nine months, I think. I've been bottle-feeding him today because even when they graze they still get some milk from their mother, but I'll try him on more solid foods, apple and corn on a cob. The pre-school class usually has guinea pigs so I'll see if I can scrounge some of their pellet food for him as well. In fact, I think I might drop him off up there so they can raise him. It's not easy juggling his feeds in between patients, and hard on him to be carted around with us.'

James felt his arms tighten on the bundle in his arms but admitted the idea made sense. He watched as she produced a small feeding bottle, a tin of formula and a measure from a plastic bag she'd been carrying over her arm.

'Is that baby formula?' he asked, reaching for the tin to read the label.

'Pet formula,' she explained. 'It's a special mixture that's proved the best for most species of kangaroo. Wildlife sanctuaries do an enormous amount of research on formulas. For example, kangaroos can't have cows' milk as their intolerance to lactose causes blindness, yet one of the human baby formulas is ideal for infant flying foxes.'

She took the tin out of his hands, measured a scoop of powder into a bottle, then added the boiling water.

'Here,' she said, handing him the bottle, 'you shake this while I mix some in a jug in case the little bugger needs a night feed.'

James stared at her in amazement.

'How many feeds a day is he on? And how do you know all this stuff?'

Harriet's smile lit up her face, erasing the lines of tiredness and strain he'd seen earlier. It also sparked something inside him, reawakening thoughts of seduction.

'I know it all because people see a first-aid post sign outside our surgery door and they bring all wounded things, human or non-human, to it. I've had to learn and that's easy—you ask the experts. I now keep a variety of animal formulas on hand for situations like this.'

'And the feeds?' he persisted, peering down at the little creature curled up in his arms.

'I've been giving them four-hourly, making six in twenty-four hours, but if he's grazing and takes solid food tomorrow I'll cut back to four.' She looked up from stirring powder in the jug and her smile widened. 'Now, when that mixture's cool enough you can feed him. I'm going to have a shower, then I'll see if I can rig up something in the back yard so the bag's low enough for him to hop in and out.'

Harriet was unique, James decided as she swept out of the kitchen, leaving him holding the baby—literally.

Harriet stood under the shower and congratulated herself on getting through another day without giving in to her body's rebellious desires. In a little over forty-eight hours James's mother would be here and the kisses would have to stop. Wouldn't they?

She thought of the kiss they'd shared this morning and shivered. Stopping had been the last thing she'd wanted, yet some instinct for self-preservation had made her move away. And mention fish!

The thought brought her back to reality, to Gold Creek and her stay-at-home genes, and she turned off the hot tap and let the needles of cold water dash against her skin for a second.

Two days, that's all she had to survive.

It proved easier than she'd imagined it would because Maud had regained consciousness and was asking for her so, having left Walter at the school—much to the delight of the children—she arranged for a neighbour to give James a lift back to Gold Creek after Thursday's Hillview clinic. When it was over he went one way and she the other, driving into town, staying overnight and returning to Hillview the next morning.

But she couldn't hide away for ever, and on Friday afternoon as she drew closer and closer to Gold Creek the internal excitement she'd hoped might have died came back in full force, making her feel almost ill by the time she reached the house.

Again the lights were on inside and James was cooking dinner, but he was different somehow, subdued—as if he, too, had used their time apart to speak firmly to his body. Only he had won where she had lost.

'So, how was Maud?' he asked when she came down from her shower in the old tracksuit she should have worn last Friday.

'They've offered radium treatment to reduce the size of the tumour and she's decided to have it,' she told him, her pleasure in Maud's decision lifting her spirits enough to allow a small smile. 'Seems Bert threw a tantrum and told her she'd never been a quitter so why the hell was she giving up without a fight this time.'

James turned from the stove where he had something that smelled delicious simmering in her big frying pan.

'Bert threw a tantrum?' He lifted a hand to illustrate Bert's height and added, 'Little Bert?'

Harriet found her smile was coming more naturally now.

'And, according to the nursing staff who see the odd tantrum so can judge, it was a beauty! The problem is she'll have to go down to the city and they're likely to be away for a few months so I'll need to find someone willing to live in the cottage over winter. I can feed the hens but I can't keep up the bits of gardening and dusting that need doing to maintain the place.'

James had turned back to the stove and she stared at his back for a moment. It was such a strong-looking back, wide at the top and narrowing to his waist, which the bow of her lilac apron only served to emphasise.

'How's Kate?' she asked. 'Did the lab phone through test results?'

'They were negative, but I saw her this afternoon and she's developing the symptoms of glandular fever—sore throat, swollen glands, headache. It's a virus that doesn't show up in blood tests until about ten days after the initial infection so we may have tested too early. All she can do is rest and I'm sure Betty will see to that. She's already co-opted half the village to take turns looking after Shaun, saying they can't afford to have him near Kate.'

'But she could have passed it on before she knew she had it,' Harriet objected, and James grinned at her.

'You can tell Betty that, if you like—*I* certainly wasn't going to, but I'll check him each time I see Kate, just in case!'

Harriet felt his smile warming her insides. She wanted to tell him not to smile at her like that, but found she wasn't strong enough.

'And Mrs Reynolds?' she said instead, thinking medical talk would be safe.

'She's holding on,' he told her. 'Her blood pressure was up, which could have caused the heart failure. I've tried a new drug so we'll see.'

He left the stove and stepped towards her, and the warmth inside became heat.

'She's very old—it can't be long before she dies,' he said gently.

'I know that,' she told him, rejecting his gentleness with brusque words because she knew if he took her in his arms, even to comfort her, she wouldn't have the strength to step away. 'Now, what's this masterpiece you're preparing for dinner? Can I set the table? Pour us wine? Red or white? Will we eat in here? It's a bit cold for—'

'Harriet, there's something else.'

The words stopped her flow of questions and she looked into his eyes and read the deep compassion there.

'Maud? They phoned while I was driving home?'

'It isn't Maud,' he said, coming closer so he stood directly in front of her and she could see his chest rise and fall as he breathed. 'It was something in the paper. Or did you see a paper in town?'

She frowned at him, wondering how on earth something in the paper could possibly affect her.

'Of course I didn't see a paper,' she said. 'I spent the evening at the hospital, took Bert out for a decent meal and talked to him until midnight, then back to the hospital this morning to see Maud, before heading off to Hillview.'

She paused, thinking back to Hillview and a slight restraint among her patients there.

'They'd have seen the paper in Hillview, though,' she said. 'The school bus brings it out.'

'And no one mentioned Doug?' James asked, and Harriet pressed a hand to her chest.

'He's been hurt? Something's happened to him? No!' she cried in protest. 'Someone would have told me!'

He took hold of her arm and shook it gently.

'He's not been hurt,' he assured her, 'but there's something else. Here!'

Reaching into his pocket, he pulled out a piece of folded newspaper and handed it to her. She unfolded it with trembling fingers, wondering what on earth it could be. Then she saw the photo and she chuckled, partly to hide a pang of unexpected loneliness.

'I wondered why he said it would be the last time he asked me,' she murmured to herself, then she became aware of James's tension and looked up from the photo with its dramatic headline and smiled.

'I'm sorry—I suppose the village expected me to be upset, and here you've been worrying about how to tell me.'

'You're not upset?' he demanded. 'According to Betty, everyone assumed it was just a matter of time until the two of you settled down. They'd even decided Doug had asked me to fill in for him so I could keep an eye on you while he was away. Evidently, the fact he and I went to school together reached here by bush telegraph and that made my living with you perfectly acceptable.'

Harriet shook her head and studied the girl Doug was kissing in the photograph. The headline, CUPID SHOOTS STRAIGHT, led into a story of the whirlwind romance between the Australian sportsman and a pretty female member of the American team. Doug, it appeared, was not commenting on where their future lay, merely assuring reporters that it would be together.

Together! The word made tears prickle in Harriet's eyes and she blinked furiously, but James must have seen them for he cursed softly and pulled her roughly into his arms, holding her tightly while she battled the emotion one stupid word had caused.

'I'm not crying over Doug,' she told him gruffly. 'He more or less told me this was happening on the phone the other night but I didn't listen properly. It's just Maud, and Mrs Reynolds, and losing people.'

She took the handkerchief he offered her, dried her tears and stepped away from him.

'Maud and Janet and Mrs Reynolds all fussed over me and did my mothering after my grandma died,' she said, sinking into a chair at the kitchen table. She twisted at his handkerchief as she went on. 'My mother was one of the family nomads, you see. She hated Gold Creek, hated the country, so she took off for the city as soon as she was old enough to leave school. Like Shaun, I was an accident. She didn't even realise she was pregnant until it was too late to do anything about it so she went ahead and had me, then brought me home to my grandparents and took off again.'

'And your father?' James asked, putting a glass of wine on the table in front of her then stepping back as if his presence might interrupt her story.

'She never said a word about him except that he couldn't marry her. He was possibly married already. I have no idea.'

'And you've never wanted to find out?'

'No,' Harriet admitted. 'I did want to find my mother, though, but for all the wrong reasons. I'd been so angry, not because she'd abandoned me—because I never felt abandoned—but angry that she hadn't come home to see Grandma when she was ill, or visit Pop who'd loved her with the same unconditional love he gave to me. Then I found her, and two weeks later she was dead from an overdose and I'll never know if it was deliberate or not.'

The tears began again and she mopped at them with his handkerchief, but now she'd started this story she found she had to keep going.

'I knew I wanted to be a nurse from the time Grandma was ill and I used to help the old district nurse we had at the time, but I knew Pop was terrified about me going to the city to train. I knew he felt I'd never come back.'

'Yet you went,' James said, and she looked up to give him a watery smile.

'He insisted,' she said. 'Reckoned I'd never know if I was a true stay-at-home Logan until I'd actually been somewhere else.'

James stared at her, feeling her pain as she peeled off the layers of scar tissue that had lain over her emotions for a long time. He'd admired her from the start, had been attracted to her as well, but now he wondered if—

'Pop died in my final year. He had a heart attack down by the creek one day and it was hours before anyone found him.'

Once again she looked at him, such agony in her lovely eyes that he felt his heart squeeze painfully. 'He never knew I'd discovered I was a stay-at-home,' she finished, and James reached down and took her in his arms, lifting her so he could sit on the chair and hold her tight.

'Of course he knew,' he told her, rocking her body back and forth as one comforted a child. 'He'd watched you grow up so he must have known. Everyone in the village knows. Heavens, I've only been here for a fort-night, and even I know.'

His arms tightened as the hand clutching his heart squeezed a little harder, but he refused to ask himself why this admission should matter.

CHAPTER ELEVEN

HARRIET knew the instant comfort had turned to something else but she didn't struggle off James's knee or move her head away from the kisses he pressed behind her ear. Instead, she shivered at the delicious sensations they generated and snuggled closer, allowing the heat to burn away her melancholy mood.

This time it was he who called a halt, lifting his head and looking into her eyes for a long moment before muttering something about the dinner.

She forced a smile to her lips and said lightly, 'First the fisho and now the dinner.' But she was glad he had stopped because she recognised a difference in his kisses, a difference that would have led them straight to bed.

They ate the meal, pasta with a delicious tomato and basil sauce, and talked of ordinary things, arguing amiably about books they'd read and music they enjoyed—finding similarities and differences in their taste. But this placid, surface conversation failed to damp down the fires started earlier. In fact, it seemed to fan the flames so Harriet felt them burning through her body and wondered if tonight they would finally be allowed to have their way and join with his desire into an ultimate conflagration.

'You're emotionally exhausted,' he said when they had cleaned the kitchen and she lingered, wanting him to take her in her arms again and not release her until they'd let their passion have free rein. 'Go to bed!'

It was an order, but she sensed its truth and walked

slowly away from him. He followed her, catching up as she reached the bottom of the steps.

'It can't be any harder for you to go than it is for me to send you,' he said gruffly, then he took her in his arms and kissed her again, the sweetest, most tender, gentle-as-thistledown kind of kiss which made her heart ache with the realisation that it was love she felt for him.

'Sleep well,' he murmured, giving her a little push to set her on her way up the stairs. 'And stay in bed in the morning. I'll bring you breakfast, if you like.'

She looked at the teasing challenge in his eyes.

'Only breakfast?' she asked, and saw desire darken them to almost black.

'Want to bet?' he said, and she shook her head. Now she knew she loved him, staying out of his bed—or keeping him out of hers—might be her only form of self-preservation.

She took the thought to bed, cold company in the lonely darkness, but once again she slept when she thought sleep would be impossible and didn't wake until the sound of voices outside drew her to the window.

James stood on the road outside, his arms around a woman who must have just arrived in the battered old station wagon now parked behind the Jeep.

Harriet peered blearily at her watch and saw that it was ten to nine—she *had* slept in! Racing to the bathroom, she splashed water on her face, cleaned her teeth then tidied up after herself. Her other usable bedroom was on this floor and James's mother would have to share this bathroom with her.

Back in the bedroom, she pulled on her jeans and a warm shirt, and hurried out to greet her guest. She was halfway down the stairs when James and his mother came through the front door. The woman looked at her, lifted her hand to her chest and said, 'Why, Rosemary, I didn't realise you were here.'

Nonplussed, Harriet halted, while James muttered explanations to his mother. The woman looked at Harriet again then turned back to her son, frowning at him quite fiercely.

'I'm sorry,' she said, moving forward at last and holding out her hand towards Harriet. 'I'm Sally Hepworth, as I'm sure you've guessed. It's your colouring—I mistook you for someone else there for a moment.'

Someone you knew quite well—someone you linked to your son, Harriet thought as she made polite noises and offered to show Mrs Hepworth her room.

'I'll take her up,' James protested, but Harriet simply sent him a withering scowl and said, 'Perhaps you could put on coffee. Your mother must have had an early start.'

She headed back up the steps, her mind working overtime. He'd been in love with Rosemary, she guessed. That explained the testing kisses, and the word 'weird' used in conjunction with them. She looked the same— would she taste the same, kiss the same? She was nothing more than an experiment to him!

'Here's the room, bathroom's across the hall. I'm still trying to get permission to put in another bathroom so you'll have to share with me—is that all right?'

The words rolled off her tongue with a sharpness that made her new guest step back in surprise.

'Now I see you in a better light you're not as much like Rosemary as I thought,' Mrs Hepworth said, dropping her overnight bag on a chair and facing Harriet again. 'So much for an artist's eye, eh?' she added, with a smile so like her son's that Harriet's heart began to thud.

'I hope you enjoy your stay,' she managed to stammer. 'I'll leave you to freshen up. Come downstairs whenever you're ready.'

Her visitor nodded and Harriet made her escape, but at the top of the stairs she hesitated. She was reasonably certain she'd never be ready to go downstairs—not while James was still in her house. Yet she knew she had to face him—now, before the torment in her mind built barriers too big to scale.

So you pretend, she told herself. Pretend you didn't feel the sudden tension in the air, hadn't guessed at what had happened in his past and realised this Rosemary had been his lover. Good grief! Would he have compared them in bed if they'd got that far?

She marched down the steps, angry now, ready to take on the world. Well, if not the world, at least the man in her kitchen.

'Good morning!' she said brightly. 'Is your mother always up and about this early?'

He eyed her suspiciously, as if trying to guess what lay behind her determined good cheer.

'Always!' he confirmed. 'I should have warned you she was likely to arrive at the crack of dawn. I hope we didn't wake you with the car doors.'

Harriet found, to her dismay, that she had to hide a smile. His almost obsequious politeness was a match for her own, but she was certain she shouldn't be finding humour in the situation when her heart was cracking so badly she was sure she could feel the blood seeping out of it.

'Oh, no, I was awake,' she said glibly. 'I was thinking I might go to town.'

'Again?' he asked, but she ignored the question. After all, it was none of his damn business what she did.

She poured herself coffee and headed for the back door as the spacious kitchen suddenly became too small for two people.

'Harriet—' he began, but at that moment his mother swept in from the hall, proclaiming her delight over the house, its furnishings, position and welcoming aroma of coffee.

'Sit out the back with Harriet and I'll bring it out to you,' James said, and Harriet got a smile ready on her face.

Not that she needed to force a smile for Mrs Hepworth. The woman was charm personified, so naturally friendly, so quietly amusing that Harriet found herself drawn into some kind of magic circle that please-call-me-Sally wove around her. Like mother like son, she thought as she made her excuses about town and escaped.

Unfortunately, she couldn't hide for ever. She pleaded tiredness to escape James's invitation to accompany them to the hotel that evening.

'You'll miss the dance,' he prompted.

'There'll be another one next week,' she reminded him. 'And next month and next year,' she added, just to make sure he got the message that she knew where she belonged.

'It was unbelievably relaxed and the people so friendly,' Sally told her at breakfast next morning. 'And what I've seen of the countryside is so beautiful. I can't think why I haven't ever wanted to paint landscapes before this, but suddenly I'm tempted.'

'Tempted?' James asked. 'To change your career path at your age?'

His mother laughed at him.

'Old stodge,' she teased. 'A new challenge is good at any age.'

Harriet watched their interaction and her heart ached to be part of it but she knew she had to stand alone, to be strong and independent and not let this love she felt for James cast a shadow over her future.

She heard James agreeing with his mother and in a deep, serious voice begin to talk about the effect the young man had had on him, and his reawakened interest in psychiatry.

'But need you be a psychiatrist to help kids like that?' his mother asked. 'Oh, I realise you'd need a team behind you and that would include a psychiatrist, but what they need most, apart from someone who values them, is someone they can talk to more easily than a professional.'

Harriet's interest grew and James turned to her and said, 'My mother does volunteer work with homeless kids. She's been trying to get me involved for I don't know how long, hence the smug smile of satisfaction hovering around her lips.' She smiled, but chose his mother's side.

'I doubt it's a smug smile,' she argued, 'maybe just a pleased one that you're thinking of the future in a more positive way.'

His head jerked back as if she'd slapped him, but all he said was, 'Diagnosing again, Sister Logan? Wouldn't you be better getting our picnic organised?'

Picnic! She'd forgotten about the picnic! Would she have to spend the entire day with these two, woven into their fabric of family closeness?

'I'll make some ham rolls, Mum brought a cake—how about you put together some cheese and nibbles to have as appetisers?' he added, and Harriet, grateful for direction in her muddled state, rose obediently to her feet and headed for the kitchen.

'Don't think she's always so biddable,' she heard James tell his mother. 'In fact, she may be sickening for something that she didn't argue.'

Sickening for something indeed! Harriet found a platter and began assembling the 'nibbles' he'd ordered. She found herself remembering an old joke Pop used to tell about someone being told to cheer up because things could be worse. So the fellow cheered up and, sure enough, things got worse.

It didn't seem funny to her today, and she was wondering if it ever had when she realised that in her case it was true. Things were sure to get worse unless James Hepworth was called back to the city and another locum finished off his two weeks.

Her gloomy predictions proved more than true, although she knew she was the only person who actually realised how much worse. Sally Hepworth fitted into Gold Creek as if she'd lived in a small village all her life. She brought home gossip and local news long before Harriet heard even a whisper of it. She charmed Janet with praise for her garden, sat with Mrs Reynolds once a week, took Shaun for walks in his stroller and talked for hours to Kate, sharing the loss of a loved one, so Harriet heard how James's father had died one week before his son's birth through Betty, not from either of her house guests.

And now James talked to Sally about his future, not excluding Harriet, who was trying hard to exclude herself, but sharing his ideas and enthusiasm with them both. And it was Sally who first made the suggestion that perhaps Gold Creek was the kind of place where a refuge for street kids could be started, where physical challenges could be offered to them as the first step towards rebuilding their self-worth.

'It's an idea,' James said, and turned to Harriet with those golden lights of excitement in his eyes.

She looked at him and tried to hide her horror. Here she was counting off the days until he'd be gone, avoiding even the slightest possibility of physical contact with him, and now he was talking about setting up his rescue scheme for disadvantaged kids in her back yard. Not literally, of course, but close by—where she'd have to see him when he visited it, talk naturally to him, see his eyes looking into hers...

'Ever thought of selling?' Sally was saying, and Harriet dragged her mind back to the conversation.

'Selling what?'

'Your grandfather's place,' Sally said, with the kind of smile that proclaimed a stroke of brilliance. 'It would be ideal. It has the creek, the hill behind it with that great cliff. We'd have to ask the local State Emergency Service group if they'd include some of our kids in their programme—imagine them being trained then called upon for rescue or bushfire work! If that didn't give them pride in themselves what would?'

Harriet shook her head, but this negative response didn't dim Sally's enthusiasm. She merely said they'd find somewhere else that suited and continued talking, her enthusiasm so infectious that Harriet found herself drawn into plans for this place of challenge in spite of herself.

And escaping James proved harder than she'd thought. The first week was OK. Sally had accompanied them to Hillview on the initial Tuesday of her visit and had been so taken with the beauty of the little place she'd returned again to paint it. She'd also accompanied them on home visits, but by the second week she knew her way around and insisted on being independent.

So now Harriet had to hide behind a bright façade in James's presence and pretend the simmering heat between them had never been more than a mirage.

'Take the side road, we need to talk,' he ordered as she drove home from Hillview on the following Tuesday.

She thought about disobeying this abrupt command but decided perhaps some words might clear the air so she turned the car onto the side-track and headed up to the top of the hill.

'Now, tell me what's wrong,' he said, taking hold of her shoulders and turning her to face him. 'It's more than a natural diffidence with my mother being here. What is it, Harriet? What's happened to make you close up like this?'

She looked into his face and read her own desire burning in his eyes. If he kissed her now—

'No!' She felt the word erupt from within her and saw him sit back in surprise.

'No?' he puzzled, his brows drawing together in a frown. 'No, you won't tell me or no, what?'

Harriet lifted her shoulders in a hopeless shrug.

'The no was to myself,' she admitted. 'And, as to the rest, it took your mother's mistake to make me realise why you labelled your kisses "weird", to understand why you all but fainted when you arrived at Gold Creek and saw me standing there. I was someone else to you. I have been all along. This Rosemary! What happened? Did she not want to wait while you were in hospital? Did she fall in love with someone else? She was your dark misery, wasn't she? And I was a convenient substitute—obviously alike enough for you to close your eyes and pretend!'

A rising anger had carried her this far, but now something hard was clogging up her throat and the words became more difficult to pronounce, but she battled on, determined to get it all out in the open.

'Would you have slept with me, pretending it was her? Cried her name instead of mine in the throes of love-making? Not that it matters,' she finished gruffly. 'It could never have been more than a brief affair, could it?'

She looked up at James, knowing he'd see the tears she couldn't keep out of her eyes but not caring that he saw her sadness. What broke her was his voice when he whispered, 'Oh, Harriet!' When he drew her close she didn't resist, but let him hold her against his chest in the awkward confines of the car and press his lips into her hair.

'I can't deny it, Harry,' he whispered, and after a lifetime of hating the shortening of her name it sounded like a melody. 'Not any of it. In fact, there's more. It was Rosemary driving the car when I was injured, and I thought it was guilt that kept her from my bedside in those first awful weeks. But later I learnt she'd been put on the transplant team in my place, that she'd been too busy learning and working to come and see me.'

Harriet pushed away from him, reawakened anger mounting to fury.

'And you still felt bad about losing her? You have regrets about such a selfish, uncaring... Oh, I can't believe you, can't believe any of it! Men!'

Shaking with rage and frustration, she started the engine.

'What are you doing?' he demanded. 'We haven't finished talking.'

'I have,' she fumed. 'Finished talking, finished everything! To think you substituted me for a worthless piece of ambition like that Rosemary makes me want to throw up. If you ask me, you probably deserve each other!'

She spun the wheels, bounced over a tree stump and tore back down the track, ignoring his protests and orders to slow down. Reaching the road, she did slow down, not wanting to put him back in hospital no matter how he'd treated her, but her temper hadn't cooled and she pulled up outside the house but kept the engine running.

'Harriet—'

'Get out!' she said through teeth clenched so tight her jaw ached.

'You're not coming in?'

'Good guess!'

He touched her then, laid his hand gently on her arm

and repeated her name, but she looked away and said, 'Please go.' It was a plea now, not an order, as her unreliable temper failed her yet again.

They continued through the week in a kind of armed truce, and Harriet was pleased that work had turned busy and demanded more hours than usual each day. Sally was also busy, gleaning the story of Maud and Bert from friends and neighbours then suddenly turning organiser and arranging for them to have her house in Sydney while she moved into the cottage for as long as they were away.

With a speed that left Harriet breathless, she took off one morning, arranged an ambulance transfer for Maud, collected Bert and whisked him off to Sydney to show him her local scene, the shops, where public transport went and all the things he'd need to know for survival in the city. She returned with a small removal van behind her, full of easels, boards, paints and canvases.

'My new challenge!' she told Harriet proudly, then she peered into Harriet's eyes and said, 'You haven't been sleeping properly. I do hope James hasn't been keeping you up late with me gone.'

'Of course not,' Harriet assured her, not adding that it was thoughts of James, not James himself, who had been causing the sleepless nights. In fact, James had continued to be the perfect gentleman, not touching her or teasing her with kisses but weakening her resistance just by being the James who was an amusing companion or the James who made her feel a different kind of excitement when he talked of his fledgling plans for the future.

She could see and hear and feel his commitment to this idea of helping young people and sensed it was growing beyond the theoretical stage, but no more was said of where he'd set up his place of challenge, no mention made of the property she knew would be ideal.

And in the darkness of the night she began to dream

a dream where Pop's old place became a refuge, with James and herself working together to rebuild shattered lives.

It was impossible—he'd have to keep on working, couldn't run the place on love alone. He'll go back to the city and be a figurehead, a social money-raiser, giving expensive dinner parties to persuade other well-heeled souls to part with their cash.

Beside him in these dreams stood a woman with red hair, a mirror image of herself but answering to the name of Rosemary. And in the early hours of the morning Harriet would get out of bed and walk softly to the window, staring out at the sleeping village and reminding herself she was a stay-at-home Logan, but wondering if that was still true.

Didn't love involve some sacrifice? Could she find someone else to take her place, to live in the home she'd created here and care for her patients—her friends? She'd return to her cold bed with bleak thoughts for comfort.

'Not sleeping well, Harriet?'

She'd actually slept later this morning, rising in time to see the sun touch the top of the hills beyond the town. Now she stood at her window and glanced down at the cause of all her torment, standing in the middle of the road as if he owned the place. James looked annoyingly well and rested, temptingly strong and virile.

'What are you doing? Where have you been?' she demanded, while her heart hammered so furiously against her chest that she tried to still its beating with her hand.

'I haven't been—I'm going,' he said. 'I've been walking every morning, strengthening my hip and leg.'

'Getting fit for when you leave,' Harriet said quietly, though the desperation she felt made her want to scream.

'Getting fit full stop,' he retorted. 'Now, as you're up, pull on some warm clothes and walk with me.'

It was an order, not an invitation, but even the most tempting of orders had never sat well with her.

'Why should I?' she demanded peevishly.

'Because I want to talk to you,' he replied, stepping closer so that in the strengthening dawn light she could see the contours of his face, the dark shadows that hid his eyes.

'Talk to me? Harriet? Or do you simply need a sounding board for more of your ideas?' she asked.

She saw his shoulders lift and lower as he sighed.

'Talk to you—Harriet Logan,' he confirmed. 'A red-haired, blue-eyed termagant. The most stubborn, irritating, contrary, argumentative female it has ever been my misfortune to meet.'

He grinned at her and she felt her bones melt but she wasn't going to be won over by a devilish grin, no matter how her bones responded.

'Well, if she's all of that, why would you want to talk to her?'

His face became serious and he took a step closer, as if he'd like to whisper his reply. Unfortunately the distance between them made it impossible so the declaration, when it came, was loud and clear.

'Because I love her,' he said firmly, and Harriet had to hold onto the windowsill to keep herself upright.

'Like you loved Rosemary?' she persisted, wanting to believe him yet unable to let go of her suspicions.

'No, not like I loved Rosemary,' he told her, his voice rising in exasperation. 'I realise now that Rosemary was like a cardboard cut-out person, presenting an image of how she thought she should be to the world. And I fell for it because I didn't know any better—until I met the real thing, met you, Harriet. You're not only beautiful outside, you're solid gold all through. You're warm and caring and compassionate—'

'And stubborn and irritating and contrary and argumentative,' she reminded him with such a light-headed feeling of happiness engulfing her that she wondered how she'd managed to speak at all.

'All of those,' he agreed, 'but I love that Harriet, too. It's part of what makes her so special. Now it's your turn.'

Harriet frowned.

'My turn?'

'Yes,' he said firmly. 'You're supposed to say, "I love you too, James," and then you tell me all the wonderful things about me that make you love me—' He stopped abruptly, frowning in his turn. 'You do love me, don't you?'

She found herself nodding her response and saw him smile.

'Well, that's settled, then. As I was saying, you tell me all these wonderful things and then we kiss a bit and start talking about weddings.'

'Weddings?'

'Darling Harriet, your conversation is becoming a little repetitive and I'm getting a crick in my neck. Come down and walk with me!'

'Walk with me!' Harriet repeated, a silly smile teasing at her lips. The words sounded like a simple recipe for happiness—a promise for the future. But what future?

'I'm a stay-at-home Logan,' she reminded him.

He looked around and raised his hands. 'Who wouldn't be a stay-at-home in such a beautiful place as this?' he asked. 'I've already thought of that and spoken to Doug.'

And although she'd mentally vowed to not repeat another word he said she heard herself doing it again.

'You've spoken to Doug?'

'Of course I've spoken to Doug. I'll need a job to pay for all my grand ideas, not to mention our future together. And where better than right here at Gold Creek? Actually, it suits him for me to stay because he's got some adjusting of his own lifestyle to do. Now, are you going to come down here so I can give you a demonstration of how I feel, and talk about our wedding?' James demanded. 'Or am I going to have to drag my wounded leg up there to get you?'

Her smile settled more firmly on her lips. In fact, she felt its happiness sparkling in her skin and shining in her eyes.

'You'd never make it!' she teased.

'Want to bet?' he retorted, but as he moved towards the verandah she left the window and rushed down to meet him, ready to do a little demonstrating of her own.

It was a long time before they talked of weddings. Talk had been impossible as they'd held each other tightly while James kissed away the fears and tension that had twisted in Harriet's heart and darkened her soul with shadows.

Then her lips responded with all the hunger she'd been denying to herself. Desire flared, burning through her so fiercely she trembled as James's fingers brushed her breast.

'Cold?' he murmured. 'Let's continue this inside.'

'Not yet!' Harriet pleaded, afraid to move lest the magic bubble of happiness surrounding her should burst.

She pushed her hands beneath his shirt, feeling satin skin and fine silky hairs. He shivered at her touch and her excitement mounted as she realised the power of her touch to arouse him as his slightest touch excited her.

Her fingers continued their exploration upwards to press against broad shoulders, to feel the close-cut hair at the base of his neck. And her body pressed against him, gauging his reaction to her touch quite accurately and feeling her own excitement rise even higher to match it.

'If we stay here much longer we'll be run in for indecent exposure,' he muttered against her hair.

'They can't run you in, you're the doctor,' she teased, tilting her head far enough to see into his eyes.

'And an injured, still slightly useless but besotted doctor at that,' he said, his eyes agleam with so much love Harriet felt her knees buckle.

'Really?' she asked, still half-afraid to believe the miracle had happened.

'Really,' he assured her. 'I love you, Harriet Logan. I think I have from the first day I met you when you all but carried me into the surgery, scolding me all the way about male pride then accusing me of drug addiction and pretence. I should have disliked you immensely yet I found myself watching you far too closely, missing you when you weren't around. I wanted to hear your voice, to make you laugh, hoping you might like me just a little, yet all the time I felt strange about it—'

'Weird,' Harriet offered, and saw his lips curve into their familiar smile.

'Yes, weird, my love. I was beginning to wonder where the past ended and the future began.'

'And do you know now?' she asked, wanting to see the smile widen and that gleam of love again.

'I do, indeed,' James promised. 'I figured it out some time ago, but there was Doug, hovering in your background. Everyone in the town had you all but married to the man...'

He hesitated and she knew it was, as he'd said earlier, her turn.

'Doug and I were friends,' she assured him. 'Never more than that, although proposing to me had become a habit with him. I'd never have married Doug—'

'Because?' he prompted, and she felt heat rush to colour her cheeks.

'Because I didn't love him,' she said gruffly, burying her flushed face against his chest.

'And?' he pressed.

Harriet sighed and raised her head again.

'I do love you,' she whispered, words she'd never said before, coming out so huskily she wondered if he'd heard them until a faint colour tinged his cheeks and the look of awe and wonder in his face—the look of love— told her more than words could ever say.

MILLS & BOON®

Medical Romance™

COMING NEXT MONTH

TOMORROW'S CHILD by Lilian Darcy

A new start for Dr Paula Nichols and a new romance...

COUNTRY REMEDY by Joanna Neil

Why was Ross *so* appealing? And just when Heather had decided not to get involved!

CONTRACT DAD by Helen Shelton

Drew wasn't looking for a wife, Lizzy didn't want a husband—but she *did* want a baby!

A FAMILY TO SHARE by Gill Sanderson

Loving Sisters trilogy

LOVING SISTERS

Lisa Grey was a successful, extremely caring and stunning redhead. Just like her sisters, Emily and Rosalind, she had a lot to give but had yet to find the perfect partner. This first book tells how she met that man and how she fought to keep him. Coming soon are **A FAMILY AGAIN**, Emily's story, and **THE FAMILY FRIEND**, Rosalind's tale.

On sale from **11th September 1998**

Available at most branches of WH Smith, John Menzies, Martins, Tesco, Volume One and Safeway

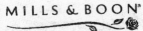

EMILIE RICHARDS

THE WAY BACK HOME

As a teenager, Anna Fitzgerald fled an impossible
situation, only to discover that life on the streets was
worse. But she had survived. Now, as a woman,
she lived with the constant threat that the secrets of
her past would eventually destroy her new life.

1-55166-399-6
AVAILABLE IN PAPERBACK
FROM SEPTEMBER, 1998

JASMINE CRESSWELL

THE DAUGHTER

Maggie Slade's been on the run for seven years now.
Seven years of living without a life or a future because
she's a woman with a past. And then she meets Sean
McLeod. Maggie has two choices. She can either run,
or learn to trust again and prove her innocence.

"Romantic suspense at its finest."

—Affaire de Coeur

1-55166-425-9
AVAILABLE IN PAPERBACK
FROM SEPTEMBER, 1998

DEBBIE MACOMBER

Married in Montana

Needing a safe place for her sons to grow up, Molly
Cogan decided it was time to return home.
Home to Sweetgrass Montana.
Home to her grandfather's ranch.

*"Debbie Macomber's name on a book is a guarantee
of delightful, warm-hearted romance."*
—Jayne Ann Krentz

1-55166-400-3
**AVAILABLE IN PAPERBACK
FROM AUGUST, 1998**

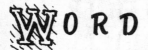ORD INK

We are giving away a year's supply of Mills & Boon® books to the five lucky winners of our latest competition. Simply fill in the ten missing words below, complete the coupon overleaf and send this entire page to us by 28th February 1999. The first five correct entries will each win a year's subscription to the Mills & Boon series of their choice. What could be easier?

BUSINESS	**SUIT**	CASE
BOTTLE	_____	HAT
FRONT	_____	BELL
PARTY	_____	BOX
SHOE	_____	PIPE
RAIN	_____	TIE
ARM	_____	MAN
SIDE	_____	ROOM
BEACH	_____	GOWN
FOOT	_____	KIND
BIRTHDAY	_____	BOARD

Please turn over for details of how to enter ⇨

C8H

HOW TO ENTER

There are ten words missing from our list overleaf. Each of the missing words must link up with the two on either side to make a new word or words.

For example, 'Business' links with 'Suit' and 'Case' to form 'Business Suit' and 'Suit Case':

BUSINESS—SUIT—CASE

As you find each one, write it in the space provided. When you have linked up all the words, fill in the coupon below, pop this page into an envelope and post it today. Don't forget you could win a year's supply of Mills & Boon® books—you don't even need to pay for a stamp!

**Mills & Boon Word Link Competition
FREEPOST CN81, Croydon, Surrey, CR9 3WZ**

EIRE readers: (please affix stamp) PO Box 4546, Dublin 24.

Please tick the series you would like to receive if you are one of the lucky winners

Presents™ ❏ Enchanted™ ❏ Medical Romance™ ❏
Historical Romance™ ❏ Temptation®

Are you a Reader Service™ subscriber?   Yes ❏   No ❏

Ms/Mrs/Miss/Mr ....Initials.................(BLOCK CAPITALS PLEASE)

Surname..

Address ....

....

....Postcode.........................

(I am over 18 years of age)   C8H

Closing date for entries is 28th February 1999.
One entry per household. Competition open to residents of the
UK and Ireland only. You may be mailed with offers from other
reputable companies as a result of this application. If you would
prefer not to receive such offers, please tick this box.   ❏

Mills & Boon is a registered trademark
owned by Harlequin Mills & Boon Limited